Was she seriously considering getting into the pool with Parker? Naked?

Why yes. Yes, she was.

But first she needed a drink. "Can we toast to our great day first?"

"That sounds great. I'll go change into my swimsuit, though. Just in case you change your mind."

"Sounds like a plan." She kicked off her shoes and padded barefoot into the kitchen, where she grabbed a bottle of white wine from the fridge, a bucket of ice and two stainless steel tumblers.

"You aren't going to swim in a skirt and blouse, are you?" Parker's low rumble of a voice came from behind her.

She turned and was confronted with the vision of him in his swim trunks, a pair of midnight blue board shorts that hung low around his waist. Looking and touching were two distinctly different things. But Parker was not a guy she was supposed to touch. Right?

* * *

The Problem with Playboys by Karen Booth is part of the Little Black Book of Secrets series.

Dear Reader,

I'm so excited you decided to get your hands on *The Problem with Playboys*! It's the first book in my new trilogy, Little Black Book of Secrets, which centers on childhood best friends Chloe, Taylor and Alexandra, and an anonymous social media account exposing the secrets and scandals of old money families like their own.

The playboy in my book is Parker Sullivan, a supersexy and überrich sports agent. Parker works hard and plays *harder.* Chloe is the first woman to fully understand his avoidance of long-term relationships. After her mother's many failed marriages, including to Parker's dad, she doesn't do commitment either. As they navigate the rough seas between them, Little Black Book makes things worse. Only love can save the day, but it'll take the course of all three books in the series to discover who is making so much mayhem in their lives.

It's a thrill ride of seduction and secrets, and I hope you love every minute of it. Drop me a line at karen@karenbooth.net and let me know if you do!

Karen

KAREN BOOTH

THE PROBLEM WITH PLAYBOYS

H HARLEQUIN®
DESIRE™

PLEASE RECYCLE
THIS PRODUCT IS RECYCLABLE

Recycling programs
for this product may
not exist in your area.

ISBN-13: 978-1-335-73545-4

The Problem with Playboys

Copyright © 2022 by Karen Booth

All rights reserved. No part of this book may be used or reproduced in any manner whatsoever without written permission except in the case of brief quotations embodied in critical articles and reviews.

This is a work of fiction. Names, characters, places and incidents are either the product of the author's imagination or are used fictitiously. Any resemblance to actual persons, living or dead, businesses, companies, events or locales is entirely coincidental.

This edition published by arrangement with Harlequin Books S.A.

For questions and comments about the quality of this book, please contact us at CustomerService@Harlequin.com.

Harlequin Enterprises ULC
22 Adelaide St. West, 41st Floor
Toronto, Ontario M5H 4E3, Canada
www.Harlequin.com

Printed in U.S.A.

Karen Booth is a Midwestern girl transplanted in the South, raised on '80s music and repeated readings of *Forever...* by Judy Blume. When she takes a break from the art of romance, she's listening to music with her college-age kids or sweet-talking her husband into making her a cocktail. Learn more about Karen at karenbooth.net.

Books by Karen Booth

Harlequin Desire

Blue Collar Billionaire

Little Black Book of Secrets

The Problem with Playboys

The Sterling Wives

Once Forbidden, Twice Tempted
High Society Secrets
All He Wants for Christmas

Visit her Author Profile page at Harlequin.com, or karenbooth.net, for more titles.

You can also find Karen Booth on Facebook, along with other Harlequin Desire authors, at Facebook.com/harlequindesireauthors!

One

Chloe Burnett came by her knack for crisis public relations honestly. She was born into it.

"Ms. Burnett, I have three things for you before you leave." Chloe's assistant, Forrest Mack, ducked his head into Chloe's office. Forrest was impossibly tall and broad. People often assumed he was a professional athlete, but he was actually an aspiring master chess player and total softie.

Chloe sat back in her chair and stared up at the ceiling. "Ugh. Right. *Before I leave.* Why does my mother do these things to me, Forrest?"

Forrest took the question as an invitation and marched into Chloe's office, immediately straightening piles of paperwork on her desk. "I don't know.

She seems like a lovely woman, but I can imagine her being quite demanding."

Demanding wasn't the half of it. The life of Eliza Burnett, Chloe's mom, was one long soap opera in which Eliza played the role of unlucky-in-love wealthy matriarch and Chloe was the unflappable workaholic daughter who could be guilted into anything. Even something as ridiculous as riding all the way out to Long Island on a Friday, and then *all* the way back, simply because her mom couldn't bear to face her soon-to-be ex-husband, but also didn't trust him to ship the last of her belongings.

"She's going to owe me for this, big time."

Forrest nodded in silence, which was basically a reminder that Chloe said that all the time and never, ever called her mom on the debt. "The three things?"

"Yes. Go." Chloe closed her laptop and shoved it into her eggplant leather Prada computer bag.

"Thomas Henley's publicist wants to move your nine o'clock breakfast meeting on Monday to eight-thirty on Tuesday. And we got the security camera footage of Dakota Ladd. She's definitely shoplifting, but you should probably watch it for yourself."

Chloe drew a deep breath in through her nose and got up from her desk. "The meeting time change is fine as long as it fits into my calendar. As for Dakota, set up a call with her manager. I think we might need to send her to rehab for another thirty days. Even if it doesn't do any good, it will at least look like she's doing something to get better."

"Got it."

Chloe breezed past Forrest. "Wait. What's the third thing?"

"Liam has the car ready downstairs and there's a cinnamon coconut milk latte waiting for you in the back seat."

"Thank you." Chloe smiled up at her amazing assistant. "I'm going straight to a bar after this little errand, so no need to wait for me to come back to the office. I hope you enjoy your weekend."

"You, too, Ms. Burnett."

Chloe strode through her office, acknowledging her employees with a nod of her head. Her team was up to thirty-two people and her firm, Burnett PR, was growing every day, in part because there was no shortage of crises in the world of business and entertainment. If all went well, she'd work like crazy until she was fifty, sell the company and retire on a beach somewhere. Crisis management wasn't her dream, but she was incredibly good at solving problems. So good that she garnered top dollar.

Chloe punched the button for the elevator and rode down to the parking garage, where her driver, Liam, was quick to open the door of the black SUV. She climbed inside and a flutter of happiness went through her when she spotted the coffee cup waiting in the cup holder next to a bottle of cold water. Forrest was an angel.

She got settled then went right to work making calls, sending emails and watching the dreaded security camera footage using the car's mobile Wi-Fi. Dakota had been a working actress in Hollywood since she was five years old and it had done a real number on her sense of self. She was prone to all sorts of bad behavior, but the shoplifting was the most persistent problem. When someone was paid seven million for a film, it didn't look great when they were caught stealing ten-dollar earrings from a chain store at the mall. As near as Chloe could tell, Dakota was crying out for help. But Chloe was not a psychologist and Dakota always dismissed Chloe's pleas for her to find a less troublesome hobby, like meditation or knitting.

Chloe's phone buzzed with a text from one of her best friends, Taylor Hayes. Taylor and Chloe, along with Alexandra Gold, had been best friends since they were at prep school together in Upstate New York—The Baldwell School for Girls. There they'd spent six years together, confiding in each other, getting into trouble and becoming impossibly close in the process. It had been twelve years since graduation, but they were still as thick as thieves. Coming from similar old-money families made it easy to understand each other, and all three of them living in Manhattan made it possible to remain close.

I can't believe you didn't tell me about @Little-BlackBook. Taylor sent through a link to a social media account by that name.

It was Chloe's job to have her finger on the pulse of anything and everything. Being at the top of the crisis PR game meant she couldn't afford to be out of *any* loop, big or small. But she had no clue what this was about. Haven't heard of it. Chloe figured it must be inconsequential. If anyone cared, she would've already been up to speed.

Seriously? Everyone's talking about it.

Even more perturbed, Chloe pulled up the account. The profile picture was simple—two letters in gold leaf against a black background—SA. The bio was short, but cryptic. *I could have been a scandal. Instead, I was hidden in plain sight. Now it's my turn to spill secrets. Every last one will be revealed.* The follower count next caught Chloe's eye—nearly one million. That was a hell of a number for one post, especially when there was no big name attached to it. What was this? A stunt? The single post gave only the tiniest sliver of additional information—the gold letters were from the cover of a black leather-bound journal. The book was worn at the corners. Quite possibly old. Not inexpensive. In truth, it looked like the most benign thing in the world. But then Chloe read the caption: "If you run in rich and powerful circles, you might want to look over your shoulder. @LittleBlackBook probably has dirt on you already. If not, I'll get it."

A chill zipped along Chloe's spine. Who was behind this? And what did those initials—SA—mean? Chloe was indeed intrigued, but that feeling was accompanied by a distinct sense of dread. It sounded as if somebody somewhere was about to have their secrets dragged out into the light. She felt for them. She consoled people like that all day long, then tried to help them figure out what to do with their lives. How to move forward. Then again, if there were rich and powerful people about to have their dirty laundry aired, it might mean new clients for Chloe.

Interesting. Thanks for sending.

The three dots that meant Taylor was typing immediately appeared. Are we still having drinks tonight?

I think so. On my way to my mom's soon-to-be ex-husband's house on Long Island. Retrieving the last of her things.

That's two hours each way! Can't she pay someone to do that?

It's my daughterly duty.

Oh right. Are you meeting your stepbrother?

Her stepbrother was Parker Sullivan, an arrogant sports agent with the client list, bank account and movie-star good looks to back it up. A total playboy. They'd never met. Chloe's mom's marriage to Parker's dad had been *that* short. Chloe had done plenty of snooping online though, and she could admit that she'd perused more than a few of his photos. From a purely subjective standpoint, the man was awfully nice to look at. I think so, she replied to Taylor.

Good luck. Call me when you're done. I need that drink!

Will do.

Chloe decided she should text Parker to give him an update on her arrival. Her mom's divorce lawyer had given Chloe his number, but Chloe and Parker had not yet communicated.

Hi Parker, this is Chloe. I'll be at your dad's house in a little more than an hour. Would appreciate it if you could have my mother's things ready. She wanted to make this as fast as humanly possible.

Sure thing, sis.

Chloe narrowed her eyes at her phone and quickly tapped out a reply. I'm not your sister.

Sorry. Step-sis.

Chloe hadn't even met Parker and she'd already formed an opinion of him. Yet another impossibly good-looking rich guy with absolutely nothing to lose. Not for long. The divorce is final soon.

But not yet.

"What a jerk," she said, knowing that Liam would never answer. Apparently everything she'd ever heard about Parker Sullivan was true. Chloe didn't want to think about what it was going to be like to meet him face-to-face. She had a well-documented weakness for cocky guys. She could hear Taylor and Alexandra scolding her. *Stay away, Chloe. Stay away.*

An hour later, they'd reached the ultraswanky enclave of Sagaponack. Chloe had been out to this part of Long Island many times, mostly for summer parties in the Hamptons. She wasn't particularly impressed by the miles of pristine lawn, the sprawling estates and the grand homes, but that was only because she'd grown up around this much wealth and opulence. It wasn't that she didn't appreciate the finer things—she absolutely did. It was more that the shiny veneer could only hide so much. In the end, all families had common threads. Secrets. Deceit. If you were lucky, love or kindness. But money made everything more complicated, and the folks who lived out here had decades-old piles of it.

Liam pulled up to a wrought iron gate, entered the temporary passcode they'd been given and began the drive down the crushed-stone driveway. On either side were manicured hedges and stretches of bright green grass as far as the eye could see. Ahead was the mansion owned by George Sullivan, Parker's father. Generations of Sullivans had lived here, all of them financiers and bankers. Chloe appreciated that Parker had broken free of that mold and gone into a different line of business. Score one for Parker.

Liam brought the car to a stop in front of a grand entrance with wide stone steps and a towering double front door. He hopped out and rounded to Chloe's side of the car, opening her door. She swung her legs around and took Liam's hand, but Chloe wasn't particularly tall and it was a bit of a drop down. Her skirt hitched up her thigh a little higher than she would have liked. Her feet landed on the rocky driveway, her heels teetering on the uneven surface. She quickly straightened her clothes, then looked up only to see Parker standing in the doorway. His thick chestnut brown hair, impossibly sculpted features, and penetrating blue-gray eyes were even more impressive in person. But it was the smirk that really caught her eye. He'd seen that whole mishap with her skirt. And he'd loved every second of it.

Parker hadn't anticipated getting such an eyeful of Chloe on their first meeting. That glimpse of her creamy thighs definitely had everything in the vicinity of his hips running hot. Even better, her cleavage when she bent forward to straighten her skirt—she wasn't busty by any means, but what she had was perfect. He could imagine them fitting just perfectly in his hands.

She was pure poetry in motion as she strode toward the front door, hips swaying in that tight skirt, lithe legs shown off with a pair of criminally sexy sky-high heels. He'd seen photos of Chloe, every one of them showing a very pretty face, big brown eyes and lush red hair. But the flesh-and-blood version of her was a total bombshell. It was like she'd been downloaded from one of his fantasies, the sort of woman he dreamed up in his head when he didn't have female companionship but still needed a release.

"You must be Parker." She ascended the staircase like a goddess, but he could also tell from her tone that she was exactly like every type-A rich girl he'd ever met—a little uptight and just begging to be unraveled. He loved the challenge of that. He lived for it.

"And you must be Chloe." He reached out his hand to shake hers. For a moment, they stood there, palms touching and looking into each other's eyes. The electricity between them was immediate and a bit shocking. Parker had chemistry with lots of women. But he'd never been former stepsiblings with any of them.

"Do you want to bring me my mother's things or should I come inside?"

"Right down to business, then?"

"Yes. I'm meeting a friend for a drink back in the city. I don't want to be late."

Parker stood back and invited her in with a sweep of his hand. "That's too bad. It seems like we should get to know each other at least a little bit. My dad was married to your mom, after all."

"For just under eight months," Chloe said, stepping inside and turning back to him. "A blip on the map for my mom, I'm sorry to say."

"I hear you. My dad's marriages keep getting shorter. It won't be long and he'll be asking his lawyer to draw up divorce papers during the engagement party. But he still insists on getting married. I don't get it. Why bother?"

Chloe slid him a look that said she was surprised by his insight. "That's exactly what I keep asking my mom. Why allow yourself to get entangled in someone else's life? Just sleep with the guy, go to parties with him and on nice vacations. It's not that hard to keep things casual, is it?"

If only she knew how much she was turning him on right now. "I totally agree. One hundred percent."

Chloe looked around the foyer, her gaze landing on the box sitting on one of the antique upholstered chairs flanking a marble-topped chest of drawers that had been in Parker's family for generations. "Are those some of my mother's things?"

"That's everything."

"What? No. That can't be possible."

"That's all there is. A framed photograph of you, a few bottles of perfume and some jewelry. My dad loves to buy women jewelry. He's such a sap."

Chloe's shoulders dropped slightly and she shook her head. "How I love the fact that she sent me all the way out here for a box that could've simply been put in the mail."

"Well, look at the bright side. My dad did the same thing to me. He didn't trust one of his staff to deal with this and he wasn't willing to do it himself."

Chloe turned back to him and smiled. It sucked the breath right out of him. "You know, that does actually make me feel better. Just knowing that I'm not the only one in this boat."

Parker spread his arms wide. "Welcome to the boat. We have hot and cold running parental guilt, sizable trust funds, all the bourbon you can drink and, if you're lucky, a big fat inheritance when it's all said and done."

A quiet laugh left Chloe's lips. "Very clever. And quick. No wonder people say you're murder to negotiate with."

Parker felt a flush of heat color his cheeks. He stuffed his hands into his pockets and looked down at the ground. "I do right by my clients. That's all."

"You just signed Marcus Grant, didn't you?"

Parker was intrigued that she knew any details of his business at all. "Do you follow sports?"

"Not football. I'm more of a basketball girl. But I know lots of alumni from the prep school Marcus attended. It's not far from where I went, and I do follow the news, very closely. Occupational hazard."

"Ah. I see. Well, good to know word has gotten around about Marcus."

"His star is really on the rise. Big rookie contract, even bigger signing bonus, multimillion-dollar endorsements."

His attraction to Chloe was only growing. "Wow. You really pay attention, don't you?"

She shrugged. "I never know when there's a potential new client around the corner. Athletes do have a habit of getting themselves into hot water."

Parker shook his head with as much vigor as he could muster. He felt fiercely protective of his biggest client. "No way. Not Marcus. The guy is clean as a whistle. Works like a beast, doesn't do the club scene, goes to church on Sunday. He doesn't drink or do drugs or any of the stuff your clients do."

Chloe frowned at him and crossed her arms. In the world of body language, she was shutting herself off from him, but he didn't see it that way—his eyes were only drawn to the gentle swell of her breasts. "Some of my clients are innocent of the things the tabloids or press accuse them of. And even when they've committed an actual crime, no person is a saint. Being a celebrity, in particular, can be very stressful. The entire world is watching, all the time. It's impossible to not have even a small hiccup."

"Not for Marcus. He's on the straight and narrow, and cashing in on his immense talent."

"Meaning you're cashing in as well."

Parker shrugged. "Of course. I'm his agent. You know, even if my client wasn't so straitlaced, I don't understand the obsession with having a perfect reputation. So what if you did something wrong? Let it go and move on. The rest of the world will do that eventually."

"That's not always true. A person's reputation is immensely important. It can impact their professional life, their earning potential, their family. It can even make their love life a nightmare. Damage control is a worthwhile pursuit."

He still wasn't done shrugging off Chloe's argument. "I don't see the point."

A frustrated grumble left her throat. Parker found it incredibly sexy. He wanted to know if he could kiss away that noise. Claim her mouth with his and make her forget why she was mad. Or even better, take it out on him in bed. "That's my entire business. You don't see me insulting your career."

"What's there to criticize about being a sports agent? It's an entirely legitimate line of work. One with decades of history, I might add."

"I assure you my business is totally aboveboard."

"I'm not saying it isn't. If you can convince people to give you piles of money for what you do, more power to you."

Chloe walked over to the box and picked it up. "I'm leaving."

Parker held out his arms. "Here. Let me carry that for you."

Chloe turned away from him, leaving the box out of his reach and Parker with a nose full of her heavenly perfume. "I'm fine. I can handle it on my own."

Parker wasn't about to fight with her. He knew he'd annoyed her with his commentary about her career, but he was just being honest. He wasn't going to adopt an opinion that wasn't his own simply because he wanted to make her feel better. "Whatever you say."

She marched off to the door, but quickly seemed to realize that she couldn't hold the box and make a graceful exit on her own. Parker hustled over to turn the knob for her. His chest brushed her shoulder. Another shock ran through him. He loved that he'd stirred up her anger, but the attraction was still there. That was the stuff of a red-hot connection. Dry kindling just waiting for someone to strike a match. "Goodbye, Parker," Chloe snapped as she stepped out onto the landing.

"Bye, Chloe. It was nice meeting you. I hope we run into each other sometime soon."

"Yeah. Right." She didn't bother to look back at him, simply rushed down the stairs as her driver ran around the side of the car to retrieve the box from her.

Parker stood in the doorway, watching Chloe climb into her car. Damn, she was so much more beautiful in person than he'd bargained for. In some ways, it was a good thing that they hadn't met until the divorce between their parents was close to its conclusion. He would've struggled with the attraction between them much more when she really was his stepsister, even if it had only been on paper.

Chloe's car pulled away, and Parker closed the door and went to make himself a drink. He'd just dropped the ice cubes into his glass when he got a text. Was it from Chloe? The thought filled him with a distinct sense of satisfaction. He fished his phone out of his pocket.

It wasn't Chloe.

The message was from Marcus. We have a problem.

Two

Chloe stewed in the car for the entire two-hour trip back into the city. Work was only a small distraction, which told her all she really needed to know—Parker had knocked her off her game. Nothing and nobody was capable of keeping her from her work. But he had. Somehow.

Parker was like every handsome rich guy she'd ever met—an endless supply of unbridled confidence that only served to fuel his good looks. The cockiness just radiated off him, and Chloe was mad at herself for letting it do things to her. Her entire body felt restless, like an abundance of energy was pent up inside her. Of course, she knew what that really meant... It was all sexual frustration. It had been months since she'd been with a man and desire was coiled tight inside her. She longed for the touch of a man like Parker.

Except not Parker. Because that would be wrong. And her mother would go absolutely berserk.

Liam dropped Chloe at the restaurant where she was set to meet Taylor. "Just call me when you're ready, and I'll be back to pick you up," he said after he opened the door for her.

Chloe hooked her favorite Hermès handbag on her arm and lowered herself to the sidewalk. "Actually, if you can just take my laptop and work stuff back to my apartment, I'll grab a cab. Then you can go home and see your family."

"Are you sure, Ms. Burnett? It's my job to be here for you."

"It's also your job to be there for your wife. How long until the baby is due?"

"Two weeks."

"Exactly. Go home."

"Will do, Ms. Burnett. Have a good weekend."

"You, too." Chloe made her way inside, immediately spotting Taylor at the far end of the bar, more than halfway through what Chloe guessed was a dark and stormy, Taylor's usual drink order. Taylor was a striking beauty, with a dark-rooted, blond chin-length bob and flawless complexion. Her brown eyes were nearly dark as night, and that matched her personality as well. Taylor was smart and kind, but she was also perpetually frustrated, always looking for the thing that might finally make her happy.

"There she is," Taylor said, hopping down from

her barstool to give Chloe a hug. Taylor was wearing a short black peplum jacket with boyfriend jeans and heels, an edgy look Chloe wished she had the guts to pull off.

"How are you?" Chloe asked, sitting on the barstool next to her friend.

"It's Friday and I'm nearly done with my first drink. Things could definitely be worse." Taylor slurped the last of her cocktail and rattled the ice in the glass. "Do you want the same?"

Chloe wasn't hard to please. "Sure. Can we order some food, too? I'm starving."

Taylor flagged the bartender, who came right over. He was exceptionally tall with a supersexy bald head, and flashed a smile that could cause a power outage. "What can I get for you ladies?"

"Two of these," Taylor said as she pushed the glass closer to him. "Plus an order of truffle fries."

"And one of those flatbreads with the mushrooms and fresh mozzarella," Chloe added.

"Coming right up," the bartender replied. "Flag me down if you need anything else."

Taylor returned her attention to Chloe. "What's your take on Little Black Book? The link I sent you earlier today?"

"What's your deal? You're obsessed."

She shrugged and tucked her hair behind her ear. "You know I love controversy. Especially if it means it might take down some rich and powerful people."

"That seems a little odd coming from you. Your

entire family is rich and powerful. What if they end up in the crosshairs?"

She dismissed it with a wave. "I'm not worried about it. My family's secrets are boring. Like the affair my grandmother had with her landscaper."

"Did that really happen? I know everyone jokes about it, but she always seemed so sweet."

"It really happened. She was getting even with my grandfather."

Another example of marriage and commitment falling apart. In Chloe's experience, it happened more often than not. "Wow."

"Plus, if you saw her landscaper, you would totally get it." Taylor laughed quietly as the bartender delivered their drinks. "Cheers." She raised her glass.

"What are we toasting to?"

"Friendship? It's the only thing in my life that ever seems to stay stable."

"To friendship." Chloe clinked her glass with Taylor's, but she had a feeling where this was going. Taylor had struggled mightily since college to find a job or career path she found satisfying. It had been a similar story with her love life. She attracted men like flies, but so many had broken her heart. It was another reason Chloe was very choosy and didn't keep anyone around for too long. "Is there something you want to tell me about?"

Taylor sighed. "Could you tell from the tone in my voice that things aren't great?"

"Is it your job or a guy?"

"It's work. I'm staying away from men. You know that. It was my New Year's resolution."

"It's March. Most people have broken their resolutions by now." Plus, she knew as stubborn and determined as Taylor could be, she never managed to stick to her guns on that one.

"Not me." She took another sip of her drink. "No, my misery is all work related."

"Anything specific?"

She shook her head. "It's the same thing that happens every time. I decide to try something and I fail. I'm not good at being an events planner, just like I wasn't good at financial services or being a fashion buyer or being a personal assistant."

"I'm sure you're better at it than you think you are."

Taylor shrugged and stared down into her drink. "I just want to be good at something. That's all. Like you. You're a badass. I'd give anything to have a career that I was great at and gave me purpose."

All Chloe could think about was her conversation with Parker and the ways he'd argued the exact opposite of Taylor's point. "Not everyone thinks it's so great."

"Like who?"

"Like my soon-to-be former stepbrother."

Taylor's face lit up. "Oh, my God. Parker Sullivan. You just came from seeing him. Is he a jerk? I've heard stories."

"He said horrible things about my job. He thinks crisis management is pointless."

Taylor arched both eyebrows. "Seriously? It's not like he's curing cancer. He's a sports agent."

"You're so right. Where does he get off saying anything about what I do? At least I help people. He negotiates sneaker contracts."

The bartender stopped by to deliver their food. "Can I get you ladies anything else?"

Chloe munched on a few crispy fries. It was sheer salty heaven. "I think we're good."

"I'll check back in a minute or two." He turned and looked up at the TV hanging on the wall above the bar. For a moment, he was frozen as he stared at the screen.

Chloe's sights were drawn to the vision of a cable news anchor and a photo of Marcus Grant. With the sound turned down, she couldn't hear what was being said, but the crawl at the bottom of the screen told at least part of the story. *Rookie's multimillion-dollar contract in jeopardy. Social media account Little Black Book leaks photos of mafia card game.* "Holy crap. That's Parker's star client."

Taylor looked up and pointed. "See? Little Black Book. I told you this was a big deal."

Chloe grabbed a few more fries, unable to look away from the TV. She wasn't sure who was behind Little Black Book, and she hated to see Marcus Grant in hot water, but, wow, was the timing ever spectacular. She imagined Parker pacing the floor of his father's fabulous home, furious over what had just happened. Would he really be able to laugh it off the way he'd suggested to her hours earlier? Or would he swallow his pride and try to get his big client out of this predicament?

"Something tells me Parker Sullivan might regret poking fun at your career," Taylor said. "Are you going to call him and offer to help?"

Chloe stirred her drink, watching the ice cubes swirl in the glass, wondering why the notion of talking to Parker made her even the slightest bit excited. "Nah. I think I'll wait and see if he decides to come to me."

Parker had signed Marcus Grant because every time he took the field, there was ice water running through his veins. Cool and calm under pressure, with a laser-guided missile launcher of an arm, he was poised to become the best pro quarterback in half a century. Away from the field, the young man was a pussycat—easygoing and friendly, with a million-watt smile. In either situation, Parker saw Marcus as completely unflappable. But two days ago, Little Black Book had rattled Marcus's cage, and he was slowly becoming unhinged.

"I don't understand who's behind this. That's what's driving me crazy," Marcus said over speakerphone.

Parker listened, pacing in his office on the 87th floor of the Manhattan high-rise his sports agency occupied. He'd nearly worn a path in the carpet since 9:00 a.m. Not good considering it was only ten. "It's got to be one of the tabloids. Some sort of social media stunt." In truth, the notion of an invisible enemy was driving Parker crazy, too. He wanted to know who or what he was fighting against. But it was all cloaked in secrecy. For the moment. "The identity of Little Black Book is not the problem. What it's done to your career is the real issue."

"But how did they get photos of me at the card game? We had to turn over our cell phones. Those men take poker very seriously."

Parker didn't blame Marcus exactly, but his star client never should've put himself in the situation in the first place. A secret high-stakes card game with men linked to organized crime was simply not a good life choice. The fact that Marcus had bet—and lost—an entire year's salary from his rookie contract? A $1.4 million loss, to be exact? That was salt in the wound.

The real problem was that Marcus was signed to Miami. The team had gone through major drama three years ago with multiple players finding themselves embroiled in four separate headline-grabbing scandals. The team became a fixture in the tabloids, which led to endless speculation about management, ownership and what exactly was going on with the franchise. It had taken that long to rehab the team's image, and Marcus was an essential part of turning the page. He signaled the fresh start they needed. The owners, the Bratt family, had been crystal clear when they signed Marcus. They wanted players who were in the headlines for big wins, not epic personal failings. They wanted players of "high moral character." They'd used those exact words. More than once.

Parker knew in his heart that Marcus was a good guy. He'd simply made a colossally stupid mistake.

"I have no doubt that they take it very seriously. You've already paid up, haven't you?" Parker asked. The last thing any of them needed was a mobster showing up looking for his money.

"Yes, sir."

"And you're never going to do this again?"

"I swear."

Parker drew in a deep breath through his nose and collapsed into his desk chair. "Okay, then. Now it's time for me to figure out how to fix this. It's been two days and it's clear that Little Black Book is not going to let this go." It turned out that Marcus came by his proclivity for gambling honestly—his grandfather ran an illegal underground casino in the 1950s. Parker never would've known about any of it if Little Black Book hadn't shared this sliver of the Grants' past last night.

"You don't think I've ruined my career, do you?"

"No. I don't. You'll prove yourself on the field in the fall. But it's not good to be in the doghouse with ownership. And you should be prepared for problems this summer during training camp. You need to walk in on the first day and figure out a way to be the rookie quarterback on a team of seasoned veterans who have already been through a lot. This is going to ding your credibility with those guys. They're already jealous of your signing bonus."

"I'll call every one of my teammates and apologize. And maybe we should set up a dinner with the Bratts. Remind them that I'm solid."

These were all good ideas, but Parker knew that the problem was much larger than that and they couldn't handle it with a scattershot approach. They needed to be methodical, especially since they had no idea what Little Black Book might do next. Parker needed an expert. "Let me come up with a plan and I'll call you when I've figured it all out, okay?"

"Okay."

"Until then, continue to lay low. Stay home. Watch TV. Work out. And definitely no more card games."

"Yes, sir."

Parker hung up and kneaded his forehead, hoping to ward off a stress headache. It was no big secret who he should call. This was a job tailor-made for Chloe Burnett. Gorgeous and smart Chloe. Capable as hell in a pair of heels. Wound tight as a spring. And oh, yeah—his stepsister until the ink was dry on his dad's divorce. Chloe was going to *love* hearing that Parker had been a little too confident when explaining that a man like Marcus would never need her services. He'd been cocky and reckless. Then again, that was what strong, beautiful women did to him.

Parker grabbed his phone, only to be taunted when the screen came to life and he was confronted by the text his father had sent him when the story about Marcus made its way into mainstream news.

Isn't this your client? This is very bad for me. I've known the Bratt family for years.

Parker's father was highly skilled at making everything about him, but it still ate at Parker. He was thirty-four years old. He was accomplished in his industry. And yet his dad still treated him as though he needed to prove his worth.

I'm on it. And the Bratts have a gold mine on their hands with Marcus.

Of course, Parker wasn't on it. Not yet. And the exchange only underscored what he needed to do. It was time for Parker to do the thing he hated—swallow his pride.

Chloe answered after several rings. "I can't believe it took you so long to call." There was a distinct edge of glee in her voice—was she enjoying her bit of revenge on him? Or was it possible she was flirting?

Parker's mind flew back to their conversation at his dad's house. She'd known a lot about Marcus. She'd said it was her job to stay well informed. Of course she knew about Marcus's bad publicity. She had to. "Look, if you're going to say I told you so, I'd like to go ahead and get that out of the way."

"If I wanted to say that, I would have called *you*. The story about your star client broke two whole days ago. You clearly hesitated to reach out."

"I needed time to think."

"Precisely why you need someone like me. I don't need time to think in these situations. I act. I know exactly what to do."

"I don't make a habit of hesitating." He winced

at the defensive nature of his knee-jerk response. "But this came out of left field. I guess it caught me a little flat-footed."

"Totally understandable. I hear that all the time. That's why I do what I do. Not that you actually believe in damage control, right? I believe you said that you didn't see the point."

Parker blew out a frustrated breath. "Look. I'm sorry for the things I said the other day. It was stupid of me and I know that now. But for the record, I hate the 'gotcha' mentality of the media. I don't agree with the idea that every celebrity has to live their life on the straight and narrow. They're human. Marcus is just a twenty-two-year-old guy who made a mistake. It happens every day."

"Little Black Book isn't exactly the media. They can do whatever they want right now."

"No, it's not. It's like someone hiding in the bushes, waiting to jump out and scare you, if you ask me. Do you have any idea who or what is behind it?"

"I have no idea. It's brand new. And Marcus seems to be one of the first people caught in the crosshairs of whatever it is they're trying to do."

"How do I fight back against someone who's hiding?"

"Little Black Book isn't what you're fighting against. You're fighting the information. The narrative." She hesitated for a moment. "It gets even more granular than that, though. What you're really fighting for is control."

A tiny sizzle of electricity worked its way through

Parker's body. "I see. And how do I get control over an invisible enemy?"

"Like I said, the source isn't the enemy. The story is. And you change that by hiring someone highly skilled in the art of crisis public relations."

"Are you seriously vying for a new client right now?"

"Only if you're seriously considering hiring me."

Parker couldn't help but smile at Chloe's comeback. She was more than smart and sexy—she was quick and had a sense of humor, which was pretty remarkable considering some of the things he'd said about her profession. "I don't usually hire someone over the phone. I'd rather meet face-to-face."

"My schedule is packed."

Of course it was. Parker's was as well, but he'd been forced to drop everything to figure out how to fix the Marcus situation. "How can I make it worth your while?"

"Well, I have to eat. We could discuss it over dinner."

"It's ten o'clock in the morning. Why not lunch? Or a late breakfast for that matter. I don't want to wait to get started. Marcus doesn't want to, either."

"You're the one who sat on this for forty-eight hours. Also, it sounds like you've already decided to hire me."

Parker couldn't gain control of his lips—why did everything she say make him smile? She was *very* good at this. "Will it make me more of a priority if I do?"

"Of course."

"Fine. You're hired. Now can we meet?"

"There's paperwork to sign, Parker. A contract. And my retainer to pay."

"I'm good for it."

"I'm sure you are. But what kind of businessperson would I be if I simply took your word for it?"

"Chloe, come on. We're practically family."

"The word *practically* is doing a lot of work in that sentence and you know it."

She was relentless and Parker couldn't have been more turned on by it if he'd tried. He really should have taken his dad up on his invitation to meet Chloe months ago, right after their parents had flown to Vegas to get married. Parker didn't want to think about how much time he'd wasted not knowing Chloe. "Okay. Send over the paperwork. And I'll instruct my bank to transfer the funds."

"Perfect. So when would you like to meet?"

"Like I said, as soon as possible."

"Fine. Dinner tonight?"

Why was his heart racing at the prospect of going out with Chloe? Was it because he wanted to see her? Or was it because he didn't want to be out in public with an expert in crisis public relations when he had a client embroiled in a PR nightmare? He decided on the latter. The former was absurd. "You know, Chloe, I worry about going to some fancy restaurant and drinking wine and having a meal together. It sounds nice, but is that necessarily the wisest choice right now?"

Chloe laughed—a light and airy titter that made his heart gallop even faster. "Parker. We have work to do. We are not going to a fancy restaurant. We'll meet at my office, order in and get into it. Seven o'clock?"

Parker swallowed hard. *Get into it.* He was such an idiot. "Yes. Okay. I'll see you then."

Three

It had been half a day since her conversation with Parker, and Chloe was already questioning her decision to take him on as a client. She'd let her desire to be right get in the way of what was actually right—not becoming professionally involved with the son of the man who broke her mother's heart. Why did she do things like this? Why did she let her ego get in the way? Yes, she'd enjoyed getting the slightest bit even with Parker. And yes, it had been pure bliss to hear him say that he needed her help. But she hadn't really taken the time to think out the true ramifications of her choice.

Parker was set to arrive any minute and Chloe was having an unpleasant moment of clarity as Forrest prepared for the meeting in her office. Her mother was going to be furious with her. Eliza Burnett was not a woman who amicably walked away from a relationship, let alone a marriage. There was no "let's be friends" in her world. Either a man was in love with her and arranged his entire world accordingly, or the door was shut, the lock was turned and the key was thrown into a fire to melt and harden into a hunk of worthless metal.

"Ms. Burnett, do you need me to stay through your meeting?" Forrest carefully set out copies of Chloe's proposal on the low coffee table in her office's more casual seating area, which featured a chic pale gray sofa and two white upholstered side chairs. Chloe wondered if this was the right setting for their dinner strategy session, but it was the end of the day, she was beat and the thought of sitting in a formal meeting room was less than appealing.

"No, it's fine. I've got the plan ready to go. I'm just fine-tuning it with Mr. Sullivan. If I need anything from you, it can wait until tomorrow."

Forrest went to work setting out napkins for dinner, along with a small ice bucket filled with various beverages. "Can I be honest with you about this Marcus Grant situation?"

"Of course."

He took in a deep breath like he needed to bolster his confidence. "It might not be the worst thing in the world that the man lost a pile of money in a card game, but the ownership in Miami is ruthless. He's going to need to jump through some serious hoops to convince them he's worth the trouble."

"I forgot that you follow football."

"Especially Miami. They're my dad's favorite team and it's our one go-to topic of conversation since my mom passed away. It helps us stay connected. He's the only parent I have left. I want to be close to him."

Chloe loved Forrest's generous nature and was dismayed at her own lack of it. Her mom was her only living parent. Her dad had passed away when she was young. Why hadn't it been Chloe's first reaction to simply tell Parker no? Why hadn't she told him to hire another crisis management firm? Of course, she knew the real answer, but it wasn't something she cared to say out loud. She couldn't stop proving herself. It was this compulsion that lived deep inside her. Parker had said terrible things about her career. She couldn't pass up the chance to prove him wrong.

Forrest's phone beeped with a text. "Looks like Mr. Sullivan just walked through security downstairs."

Chloe's stomach flipped, an immediate reaction to what was on the line with her new client. There was so much that could go wrong. She might fail to rescue Marcus's reputation. Her mom might freak out about her working with Parker. Even worse, she could easily meet both fates. "I'll meet him in reception."

"I'll grab your dinner out of the fridge."

She patted Forrest on the shoulder, even though he was so tall that she had to reach pretty high. "Thank you for being straight up with me about Marcus. I appreciate your insight."

He smiled. "It's no problem."

"Lots of people wouldn't have the courage to do that, though. And you continue to prove yourself invaluable. My entire work life would fall apart without you."

Forrest arched both eyebrows at her, but the blush that fell across his cheeks was unmistakable. "You're going to give me a big head, Ms. Burnett."

"I doubt that's even possible." Chloe walked out of her office and down the hall to reception. The elevator dinged just as she arrived. Parker stepped off the elevator, and she was surprised to see him in the state he was in. Most of her clients arrived looking bedraggled, beaten down by the crisis they couldn't escape. But not Parker. His stride was confident, his half smile self-assured, perfectly framed by his dark facial scruff. It was the end of the day and his midnight blue suit looked as though he'd just come from the tailor—not a wrinkle in sight. His white shirt was still crisp, and the contrast between the two fabrics brought out the mystery in his eyes. On the surface, he seemed like a pretty open book—fearless, handsome man with the world by the throat—but there was something unknown behind the storm of blue and gray in his eyes.

"Hey there," Chloe said, realizing her tone was a bit too soft given the circumstances.

"Hey. Thanks for meeting with me." He shook her

hand, locked eyes on her and, unless she was imagining things, he pulled her closer.

A zip of heat sizzled through her and she stepped back. Why was she feeling like this? If ever a man had been on her personal no-fly list, it was Parker. She needed to get her head on straight. "Let's go to my office and get started."

"Please. Lead the way."

Chloe did exactly that, keenly aware of his presence as they made their way down the wide corridor. She had to wonder how this meeting would have been different if they'd known each other earlier in their parents' marriage. Would they be comfortable with each other by now? Or would it have made it even more awkward?

The instant she stepped into her office, she questioned her choice of meeting location. The view of the city was spectacular from her office windows, and at this time of night, the glimmer of lights against the dark night sky was beautiful. But it was a little too appealing. Romantic. Sexy, even. "Please. Have a seat."

"I'm going to get comfortable if that's okay with you." Parker didn't wait for an answer, strolling past her until he stood in front of the sofa. One by one, he rolled his shoulders out of his suit coat. It all seemed to happen in slow motion as he draped it over the back of a chair, unbuttoned the cuffs of his shirt and rolled up his sleeves, revealing a pair of incredible forearms with a careful folding of the fabric. Next went the tie as he tugged at the knot and zipped it down and out from his collar.

Chloe knew what came next—the button on his shirt. Hopefully it wasn't about to be buttons, plural, but Parker was a wild card, a complete unknown. She averted her eyes and shook her head. *Get your act together, Chloe.*

Luckily it was over quickly. Unfortunately it was two buttons. He sat and draped one arm along the back of the sofa. "Much better."

She truly was not used to seeing a client so calm and collected. People came to her when their lives were falling apart. "Great. My admin will be in with dinner any minute. I ordered from M Sushi."

"Really? It's my favorite."

"I know."

"You do? How, exactly?"

"I read an interview you did after Marcus got his big contract."

"But I only hired you this morning and you told me your day was packed."

She fought the urge to roll her eyes. "I found time for due diligence. I had to know what I was dealing with."

"But you didn't do this when my father married your mom?"

Chloe sat on the other end of the sofa and that was when she first noticed exactly how good he smelled. Like the richest notes of fine bourbon. "Honestly? It didn't even occur to me. No offense to your dad, but I didn't expect it to last."

"I am not offended. I thought the same thing."

Forrest showed up at the door. "I have dinner if you're ready."

Chloe waved him in. "Parker, this is Forrest, the best admin in the entire world."

"Nice to meet you, Forrest. You must be amazing. I have a feeling you have a very discerning boss."

Forrest shook Parker's hand. "She's the amazing one. I'm very lucky." He glanced at Chloe. "Would you like me to unpack the food?"

"I've got it," Chloe answered. "Go home and enjoy your evening."

"Will do. Nice to meet you," Forrest said to Parker. "Have a good night."

Chloe went to work unpacking the food, two beautifully arranged trays of assorted sushi, including Parker's favorite, the spicy tuna roll. "Please, take whatever you want to drink. We have water, tea, soda…"

"Beer. Perfect." He plucked an amber bottle from the bucket and wiped it down with the small towel Forrest had left. "You want one, too?"

Chloe was afraid he might suggest that, although the truth was that she could definitely use a drink. "Sure."

Parker handed over the bottle and popped a piece of sushi into his mouth. "Delicious. You've already made my day so much better."

Chloe couldn't contain her smile. It did make her happy to know that he was pleased. "Glad to hear it."

Parker picked up the packet of paper next to his

meal. "Is this your plan for taking down Little Black Book?"

Chloe narrowed her sights on him. "You mean rehabbing Marcus's image. That's what the plan is about."

"No. I mean exactly what I said. Marcus's image should be fine because in all truth, it is fine. If we unmask whoever is behind Little Black Book, isn't that simpler? Just expose them for what they are, an opportunistic entity trying to stir up trouble?"

"It never works to cast a bad light on someone else in these situations. Plus, you might not like the answer to these questions if we find out."

Parker shook his head in dismay. "I don't understand it at all and it's driving me crazy. How does a social media account break this story rather than a major news outlet? I've never even heard of it. Now I've been contacted by a million papers and cable news channels breathing down my neck for a comment."

"I don't know who's behind it, but I don't like to expend a lot of energy on things I can't control."

"Is that your thing, Chloe? Control?" He cast her a smoldering look, one that said he wasn't necessarily talking about work.

She wasn't about to let Parker derail their discussion. "When it comes to this, yes."

"Well, I had someone on my staff do some digging today and I found out that several people think the initials 'SA' on the cover of the black book stand for Simone Astley. Do you know who she is?"

Chloe did, but only because Simone Astley was a notorious figure in the high-society circles of the American Northeast, the very world Chloe had grown up in. "I don't know how that could possibly be. Simone Astley died several years ago. I'm pretty sure she had no kids. And I know she never married and was an only child. Her entire family line died out when she did."

"Doesn't mean someone didn't get their hands on her diary."

"But this card game Marcus got caught up in just happened. That doesn't make sense." This theory of Parker's was intriguing, but it was a dangerous idea to pursue. In her experience, chasing after the source of a rumor never accomplished anything good. "And if you want Marcus's name cleared, you need to stop digging. Now."

Parker let out a dismissive grunt. "If you tell me I can't do something, it only makes me that much more determined to do it."

"I'm serious. Leave it alone. You're going to make more problems that you could possibly ever solve."

He held up his hands in surrender. "Fine."

"You promise?"

A distinct frown crossed Parker's lips. "I swear."

"Please. Let's go through the plan." She pointed to his copy of the proposal she'd written that afternoon. "I think we go simple. From everything you've said, Marcus doesn't have skeletons in his closet. So let's shine a light on the good. I'd like to go down to Miami and oversee several high-profile interviews and photo shoots. We'll show off that stunning waterfront mansion he bought after he was drafted. We'll share his workout routine with a cover story in a men's fitness magazine. And we'll show off his softer side with a heart-to-heart interview with one of the premier cable news shows. We'll let him explain what happened that night at the card game. And he can talk about his family."

Parker flipped through the pages and tossed it back on the table. "That's it? I'm paying you a lot of money and that's all we get?"

"Excuse me? We're talking about positive publicity worth millions of dollars. It's the difference between some of his corporate sponsors dropping him and him picking up some new ones. Plus, I've already pulled huge favors with editors. They don't like snapping to attention just because I want something. Most important, it'll get him back in the good graces of the Bratt family. From what I understand, that is no small feat."

"I'm not sure it's worth what I'm paying you. I probably could've done that on my own. Make a few phone calls."

"The retainer also includes my time and travel down to Miami."

"You'll be there?" He popped another sushi roll into his mouth and wiped the corners of his lips with a napkin.

"Of course. I need to make sure everything goes perfectly, and I'll be on hand in case there are any problems."

"And you really think this will work? Is it really that simple?"

"For Marcus, it should be. People want to love him. We just need to push them back in that direction."

"Okay, then. We're going to Miami."

"We?" Chloe shook her head and a nervous laugh leaked out of her mouth. "You don't need to be there. You're paying me to take care of it. That's what I do."

He knocked back another swig of his beer. "No way I'm not going to be there. Marcus is in crisis. He needs to know that he's my number one priority. Where you go, I go." He pointed at her with the bottle.

Chloe sighed. She really preferred to work alone. Plus, she needed to have as little involvement with Parker as possible. She could tell her mom that she wasn't working for Parker so much as she was working for Marcus, but that argument only worked if she and Parker weren't spending time together. "You were just complaining about how much money you're paying me. You should let me do my job."

"And you should extend me the same consideration. Marcus is my top client right now, but he's young and still a little impressionable. If I'm not there for him through this bumpy patch, a lot could fall apart. My whole business."

That was when Chloe realized just how much was on the line for Parker. And she implicitly understood what it was like to want to defend everything you'd built. "Okay. Fine. As I said, I've already laid the groundwork with the publications, so I just need to tie a few things up, but we should be down there by lunch on Wednesday. Forrest will book my flight tomorrow morning. I'll let you know what time I'm arriving. As for hotel, I typically stay at the Mandarin, but you should do whatever you want."

"That's not necessary."

"Which part?"

"The flights and the hotel."

"Unless you've discovered a way to teleport to Miami, we're going to need to get on a plane. And I do like to sleep, so I'll need somewhere for that, too."

"I have a company jet. We'll take that. And Marcus has an incredible guesthouse. I've already stayed in it. Plenty of room for two."

"As in two bedrooms? Because I'm not sharing."

A devilish smile crossed Parker's tempting lips. "Actually, I believe it has four bedrooms. But I like how you're telling me up-front that you don't want to spend any time with me and you're definitely not ending up in the same bed as me."

"You're my client and technically my stepbrother. We are not sleeping together. Ever."

"You're the one who kept saying that you *aren't* my sister. Plus, that won't be a problem after tomorrow anyway."

"Why?"

"You haven't spoken to your mom? The divorce is about to be finalized."

Chloe hadn't spoken to her mom in a few days, which was unusual, but Chloe had been enjoying the respite. She adored her mother, but it took so much energy to keep up with the turmoil. "Oh. I didn't know."

"So that bit of conflict between us will be officially put, well, to bed." Parker laughed at his own joke.

Chloe doubted it could be that simple. "If you say so."

"I'll pick you up at your place on Wednesday morning. We can be in Miami by lunchtime. Where do you live?"

"I'm in Chelsea. 23rd St. A block off the Hudson. I can text you the address."

"Are you serious? I'm in Hudson Yards. The big tower. 72nd floor. We're practically neighbors."

Chloe could not believe her luck. Like she needed any more closeness with Parker Sullivan. "It's a huge city. I don't think we're really that close."

He shrugged. "Eleven blocks is nothing."

"If you say so." *Not nearly enough, that's for sure.*

Parker got up from his seat and grabbed his suit coat, slinging it over his shoulder. "Thanks for dinner. It was nice."

Chloe stood and walked him to the door. "Of course. Thanks for meeting with me. Thanks for trusting me with your client."

He took another look at her and she felt that connection again, the one that told her she shouldn't be involved with Parker. There was something about him that was too tempting. Perhaps it was because he was essentially forbidden fruit. "You know, Chloe,

I'm sorry we didn't get to know each other when our parents were married. But something tells me this is better."

"Why's that?"

He shrugged and patted her on the shoulder. "We didn't get invested in their drama. I hate it."

"Me too."

"It's exhausting. I'm just praying this was the last time down the aisle for my dad."

"It's beyond pointless, isn't it?"

He grinned. "Save yourself the heartache and just have fun. That's a far better way to go."

Four

Chloe did not manage to escape Manhattan on Parker's private jet undetected. Mere seconds after they took their seats on the plane, her phone rang. "Mom. Hi," she said when she answered. "I'm so sorry, but I can't talk right now. Can I call you back later?"

"I only need you for a minute."

Parker, who was seated across from her, quirked an eyebrow. *Mom?* he mouthed.

Chloe fluttered a hand in his direction, discouraging his attempted participation in her conversation. She shifted in the luxe white leather seat, noticing how uncommonly comfortable it was. She was used to luxury, but Parker definitely went with the very best of the best. "Okay."

"You haven't called in days."

A wave of that old familiar guilt hit her, probably because she hadn't called her mom on purpose. She hadn't wanted to face the inevitable questions about what she was working on, and that would have led straight to her involvement with Parker. "I know. I'm sorry."

"I wanted you to know it's all over. It's done. All ties have been cut."

"The divorce from George?"

Parker cleared his throat. Chloe thought about kicking him in the shin, but she didn't want to give him an excuse to insert himself into her call with her mom.

"Please don't say his name. I don't want to think about him or anything having to do with him. He's terrible. One of the worst decisions I've made in my life."

Right there was confirmation of Chloe's theory about how her mom would react to any man with the last name Sullivan. "I'm sorry. Try to think of it as a good thing. You have a clean slate now. You're a free woman. Maybe you should try staying that way for a while."

"I need to go to Paris and drown my sorrows in designer clothes and too many croissants. But I don't want to go alone. Please come with me."

"Mom, I can't. I just got on a plane for a work trip. We're about to take off. You should go have fun and text me pictures."

"Where are you off to?"

"Miami."

"That's perfect," her mother squealed. "I'll fly down there. We can spend time together when you're done working."

Chloe's heart broke out into a full-on sprint. She didn't want to disappoint her mom, and it did sound like fun, but that was way too close for comfort. "No. Don't."

"Excuse me?"

"I'm only there for one night. I'm just walking a client through a few interviews and then I'll be back in the city."

Her mother sighed. "Are you sure I can't come?"

"It's not that I don't want you to. I just can't be here for that long."

"Okay, darling. Well, I'd like to see you. Maybe I can have you and the girls over for Sunday brunch. That would be really nice for me."

"The girls" meant Taylor and Alexandra. Chloe's mom had been hosting them for Sunday brunch since summer vacations when the three friends were in their late teens. "Does that mean you aren't going to Paris?"

"It's no fun alone."

"Sunday brunch it is. The usual time?"

"Yes."

"It's a date. I'll text Taylor and Alex."

"Perfect. I love you."

"Love you, too." Chloe ended the call and exhaled, then switched her phone to airplane mode.

The pilot's voice came over the intercom. "Good morning, Mr. Sullivan. We're all clear to depart for

Miami. Our flying time will be just over three hours. We have smooth skies ahead, so just sit back and enjoy the ride."

The flight attendant stopped by. She was tall and blonde and gorgeous, another example of Parker surrounding himself with the best of everything. "Champagne after takeoff?"

"I'll have coffee," Chloe answered.

"Mr. Sullivan?" the attendant asked.

"Check back with me once we're in the air. I'll focus on getting Ms. Burnett to change her mind about champagne." He flashed a flirtatious smile at Chloe as they began taxiing down the runway. "How's your mom?" he asked as he fished his laptop out of his bag.

"I think you know the answer to that. She hates your dad."

"She wouldn't be the first. There's a long string of women before her and I'm sure there'll be more down the road."

Chloe didn't know Parker's dad, but she wasn't a fan, and Parker clearly wasn't trying to sway her. "I'm not going to change my mind about champagne, by the way. It's still morning. I have work to do." She pulled out her own computer. Three hours was a lifetime. She could get a lot accomplished.

"I didn't think you would. I just wanted to give you crap about it."

He was so frustrating. And somehow adorable, which made him even more irritating. "Remind me to return the favor someday."

After takeoff, Chloe got her coffee and Parker thankfully did not make a second attempt to coerce her into drinking something more celebratory. They worked in quiet, sitting across from each other, and it was actually quite pleasant to be with someone who took their job just as seriously as she did. A few times, she got stuck on a point in the project she was working on and needed a moment to think. That gave her the opportunity to slyly admire him. He'd taken his jacket off and rolled up his sleeves, a sure way to Chloe's heart as it gave her the chance to silently drool over his forearms.

But then he looked up and caught her eyeing him. "Change your mind about champagne?"

She shook her head with a bit too much enthusiasm. "No. It's nothing." For the next two hours, she kept her eyes on the computer screen. It meant she wasn't ogling Parker, but it also meant a headache after so much time looking at the harsh blue light. She closed her laptop and set it aside, pinching the bridge of her nose and rolling her head to ease the tension in her neck.

"Stress headache?" Parker asked. "I've got a trick for that."

Before she could answer, he was up out of his seat and stepping behind hers, reaching down and grasping her shoulders. She was about to protest when his thumbs pressed firmly on either side of her spine and his fingertips began kneading away the tightness that had bound up her shoulders. This was not a professional situation for either of them. Chloe did not allow her clients to give her massages, but, damn, it felt good. She closed her eyes and gave in to it. Maybe it was okay to let him touch her like this. Just once.

He began rolling his thumbs up and down the back of her neck, his fingers resting on her collarbone. She dropped her head forward and moaned. "That feels so good."

"Yeah?" His voice was a low and sexy rumble that Chloe could not ignore. It poked at the fire inside her, the tiny flame that could easily grow into an inferno if she wasn't careful.

"Yes. It does."

"Good. I'm glad. Just relax." He continued with his ministrations and Chloe didn't want to admit that she would pretty much do anything to thank him for making her feel this good. The stress was melting away. "You need to spend some time in the pool at Marcus's guesthouse tonight and tomorrow. It'll really help you unwind. And it's beautiful. Tucked away in a very private tropical courtyard. It's nothing short of paradise."

That sounded like sheer heaven. Unfortunately, she was not prepared. "I didn't bring a bathing suit."

"Chloe. We're going to Miami. Why wouldn't you plan on swimming?"

Because she was an idiot? He had an excellent point. "Too much work to do while we're there. I figured we wouldn't have time. We're only there for two days and one night."

"I think you'll find a way to make time when you see the pool."

"I saw photos when I did my research on Marcus and pitched the architectural magazine. That still won't change the fact that I don't have a swimsuit."

He dug into the back of her neck a little more firmly. "You can always skinny dip." This time his voice was right behind her, mere inches from her left ear.

With her eyes closed, his miracle-working hands on her skin and his sexy voice filtering into her brain, it wouldn't have taken much for her to agree to take a naked swim with Parker. It would have taken virtually no effort on his part to get her to drop her head to one side so he could kiss her neck, work his way up to her jaw, then beneath her ear and finally around to her lips. "I'm sure you'd love that, wouldn't you?"

"I'm not trying to convince you to take your clothes off, Chloe, if that's what you think. I say this for your benefit as much as mine. I need you at the top of your game over the next two days. There's no way you'll be like that if you're wound as tight as your neck is right now."

"I do my best under pressure." Still, the thought of unraveling in Parker's presence held immense appeal.

"Mr. Sullivan, we're beginning our descent," the pilot said over the intercom, interrupting her lurid train of thought. "It's a beautiful day in Miami. Sunny and seventy-four degrees. We'll be on the ground shortly."

"Time to buckle up," Parker said, taking his seat.

Buckle up. She definitely needed to settle in after

that back rub. Her shoulders were still tingling. Parker's touch was a revelation, but she was scolding herself for enjoying it so much. Why did she want more? From him? This wasn't like her. At all. She was the woman who kept her eye on the prize, and logic said that getting this job done so she could move on to the next one was not only what she wanted, it was what she needed. But there was a little voice in her head telling her that it was okay to crave his hands on her and to wonder what it would be like to kiss him. She might be focused, but she wasn't a robot. That bit of warm human attention had stirred a hunger inside her.

The plane touched down a few minutes before noon, and Parker had a driver waiting for them on the tarmac, who whisked them away in a jumbo black SUV. They sailed through the bright and sunny city as palm trees bent in the wind and slivers of blue water peeked out between buildings perched atop manmade keys. Maybe it was the change of scenery, but, damn, she felt like playing right now. Not working. *Get it together.*

When they pulled up to Marcus's Miami Beach mansion and they stepped outside, the sight took Chloe's breath away, even though she'd seen a whole slew of pictures online. It was a sprawling modern structure of glass and stucco-covered concrete set in a tropical paradise, which she knew to include eight bedrooms, ten bathrooms and an infinity pool running the width of waterfront property with an unobscured view of Biscayne Bay.

"We'll go around the side to the guesthouse," Parker said. "We can drop our things and meet Marcus inside."

"Perfect. The photographer and writer from the men's fitness magazine should be here in less than two hours."

Parker entered the code on the wrought iron gate and opened it, offering with his hand for Chloe to go first. "Straight ahead."

She started down the path, which had square gray stepping-stones with moss packed between them. Textured white walls were on either side, shutting out any sounds other than the soft trickle of a fountain and a few birds chirping in the branches above. With every step, she felt herself unwind a little more. The sights, sounds and smells of her surroundings made her want to jettison work and do nothing but play. The instant she reached the end of the path, she came to a stop. "Wow."

"Pretty impressive, huh?"

"That's putting it mildly." She didn't know which way to look first. Everything before her—the lush tropical landscaping and the serene oasis of the pool, surrounded by a clean-lined, all-glass house was simply too beautiful to be believed.

"Wishing you'd brought that bathing suit?"

She was. A lot. The pool was so inviting it felt as though she might never get beyond the regret of not bringing a damn bathing suit. "I'll dangle my legs in the water."

"Your room is on that side." Parker pointed to the far corner of the guesthouse. "I'm over here."

There was nothing but an open-air breezeway between them. And they each had a door. She was thankful for that. "I'll get unpacked and meet you back here in a few." Chloe cast aside her bathing suit woes in favor of exploring her bedroom. It was tranquil, with pebbled pale gray terrazzo floors, all-white bedding on a king-size bed and floor-to-ceiling windows on three sides that afforded her a perfect view of the tropical plants and that tempting pool area. She could see herself wanting to stay here for a very long time. She could imagine herself not wanting to go back to New York. But that wasn't reality, just like her thoughts about Parker weren't grounded in anything that made sense. And yet, they were there, crowding out things like logic and sensibility.

She needed to get her head on straight, so she forced herself to at least make good on the one thing she'd said she was going to do. She unpacked her clothes, then met Parker back in the courtyard.

He was pacing back and forth, talking on the phone. He glanced at her and bounced both eyebrows. "I need to run. I'm going to be with Marcus the rest of the day, but text me if you find out anything." He jabbed at the screen to end the call.

"Everything okay?"

"Absolutely perfect. Come on." Parker led her back through the walkway to the gate and out into the parking area outside the main house. Large rectangular slabs of bright white concrete, artfully arranged with lush green grass in the gaps, led up to an oversized double door of ebony wood. He didn't knock. He walked right in. "Hello? Marcus?"

"Mr. Sullivan? Is that you?" A man's voice came from the other room.

Parker waved Chloe ahead. "I told you to stop calling me that, Marcus. You make me sound like I'm your teacher or something."

As they walked into an open and airy great room, with a luxe living space off to one side and a large kitchen to the other, Marcus Grant came into view. He was just as all-American as Chloe had seen in his pictures, with a dazzling smile, close-cropped dark hair and warm brown eyes. His bronze skin was glowing, which was impossible to ignore since the very fit Marcus wasn't wearing a shirt.

"Oh, shoot. Mr. Sullivan. You didn't tell me you were bringing Ms. Burnett in with you." He grabbed a T-shirt that was sitting on the kitchen island and scrambled to put it on.

"Hey, Marcus. I have Ms. Burnett with me," Parker said in his trademark smart-ass tone.

Chloe extended her hand, trying to ignore the awkwardness. "Nice to meet you, Marcus."

"Sorry about that. If my mom knew that I met a woman for the first time without my shirt on, she'd kill me."

Chloe shook her head, finding Marcus's demeanor nothing short of super charming. He cared about what his mom would think. Who wouldn't love that? "Think of it this way. Your first interview is with the writer from the fitness magazine. Now I know you're just as in shape as I told them you were."

Parker snorted and put his arm around Marcus's sizable shoulders. "See? I told you she was the perfect person for the job."

Chloe took a deep breath, hoping that assessment bore out as true. Then in two short days, Marcus would be back on the road to reclaiming his pristine reputation, Chloe could celebrate a job well done and she and Parker could walk away from their professional involvement. That was all she wanted. Well, mostly. There were a few other things she wanted, but she knew that she needed to focus on what was good for her. *Not* what was tempting her.

Five

"Mr. Sullivan says you're the best at what you do, Ms. Burnett," Marcus said as they all took a seat in his sprawling living room.

Chloe shot Marcus an inquisitive look. "He does?"

Parker didn't get embarrassed, but something about Chloe made his cheeks flush with heat. "I did. I told him that I would only hire the best."

"Hmm," she said, still appraising him with those big brown eyes of hers. "Thank you. I appreciate that."

You can thank me later. He definitely had Chloe, the pool and the lack of a bathing suit on the brain. Would she be open if he made a move? He gauged his chances at 50/50, which weren't great odds. He felt as though most women he met were an open book, but Chloe? She was toying with him…warm one minute and chilly the next.

"I'd like to go ahead and do your interview prep," Chloe said to Marcus.

"You mean like feed me the answers?" Marcus asked.

"Actually, I'll feed you what I think will be the questions. And only the worst of them. It will give you a chance to practice your answers in front of Parker and me. We'll give you some feedback and you'll be that much more relaxed for these interviews."

Marcus nodded. "That sounds good."

"We don't want you caught off guard," Chloe added.

Parker's phone buzzed in his pocket several times. He needed to let Chloe get to work, but he also needed to check on what was so urgent. "Excuse me for a moment." He wandered into the kitchen while Chloe and Marcus got started in the living room. He dug his phone out of his pocket and saw two text messages. The first was from Jessica, the woman who did investigative work for Parker's agency. She was the younger sister of one of his clients and unbelievably talented at tracking down the most obscure dirt and information.

Getting closer with @LittleBlackBook. I'll keep digging.

Thank you, Parker responded. Chloe had told him to not do this, but Parker needed this Marcus story to not only die a quick death, but a complete one. He didn't want to deal with this more than once. Although the interviews and positive publicity would help, it only made sense that shutting down the source of the gossip would really buy him some peace of mind.

The second message was from his dad. Have you straightened things out with Oscar Bratt? He and I are in the same golf tournament in two weeks. I'd like to know I can talk to him without embarrassment.

How Parker hated the complete lack of faith his father had in him. It had been like this for as long as he could remember, and Parker had no idea how to fix it. All he could do was keep trying. He'll be happy with Marcus's next steps. I promise.

Are you meeting with him while you're there?

No. He's on vacation with his family.

That didn't seem to warrant another message from his dad, so Parker tucked his phone into his pocket. He was about to join Marcus and Chloe, but they were already deep in conversation and it was clear that he would only be interrupting. He pulled up a barstool at the kitchen island to watch their prep session. Marcus was clearly enamored of Chloe. Charmed by her, even. And as Parker studied her, the way she was so focused and earnest, it only made him that much hotter for her. He was still reeling from the neck rub on the airplane. He'd started it innocently enough, but the instant his hands touched her shoulders and he saw the luscious view down the front of her silky blouse, he continued out of pure selfish desire. He'd imagined her breasts in his hands, his tongue on her nipples, her perfect manicure raking through his hair. He was going to have to make at least a cursory attempt at getting her into the pool that night. Miami was his one chance at Chloe. Once they returned to New York, it would be game over.

After about an hour of prep, the crew from the men's fitness magazine arrived at the house. They started with a short interview, which Chloe and Parker observed from a distance. She watched it all like a hawk, acting as Marcus's protector, silently mouthing the answers to questions and smiling and nodding when he did well. Parker appreciated just how seriously she took her job. He also admired the view as her face lit up and she remained laser focused. She was more than sexy. She was flat-out adorable. His desire for this day to be over was growing by the moment. He only wanted to be alone with her. See if there was something there, even if it was only for one night.

The interview complete, the team embarked on the photo shoot, which included a weight session in his home gym, then things like stretches and yoga poses out on the picturesque patio near his pool. Chloe was busy during this part as well, working with the photographer and making sure they were only capturing Marcus's best angles and features. That was done by five o'clock, leaving little time for Marcus to shower and change into proper clothes for his interview with the architectural magazine. That one was a bit more of a walk in the park as they focused on Marcus's marvel of a home and not on the controversy. They were set to send a full camera team in a few days to gather the rest of the material for the feature.

By 7:30, it was back to being just the three of them. "I'm starving," Marcus said. "It was probably dumb of me to give my personal chef the day off, huh?"

"Should we order a pizza?" Parker asked as his stomach rumbled.

"I had my assistant order some Thai food. It should be here shortly," Chloe said.

"Thank you, Ms. Burnett," Marcus said. "That was really thoughtful of you."

"Please. Marcus. Call me Chloe," she replied.

Parker pulled her aside, gently gripping her arm and wishing he could touch more of her. "You really don't miss a beat, do you?"

She smiled and shrugged. "I'm just as hungry as you two. And I knew I wouldn't want to wait once the second writer left."

"Don't play it off, Chloe. You were amazing today. You didn't have to think twice about what you were doing. Marcus clearly adores you. You handled everything with both writers perfectly. They had nothing but the utmost respect for you."

"Careful, Parker. It almost sounds like you're impressed."

"I absolutely am."

She pressed her lips together and the most beautiful blush colored her cheeks. It seemed to light a fire in her eyes. It made parts of Parker's body run hot. "You are so smooth, aren't you? Is your dad this smooth? Is that why my mom fell so hard for him?"

Parker didn't want to talk about his father, but he did feel as though he owed her an answer. "Different kind of smooth. I might go so far as to say my dad can be slippery. I'm not like that. I simply don't want to let a great job go unnoticed. It has nothing to do with you being a woman. Or you being beautiful. Which I'm guessing was a big part of my dad's motivation with your mom."

She shook her head, and a lock of her hair fell across her face. "Something tells me I need to watch out for men with the last name Sullivan."

The doorbell rang, and Parker was off to collect their meal. "Nah. Only one of them."

Parker, Marcus and Chloe sat out on Marcus's magnificent patio for dinner, soaking up the setting sun, ocean breezes and the unbelievable view of Biscayne Bay. They enjoyed red curry with chicken, green curry with shrimp and summer rolls with rice noodles and fresh mint. Marcus was noticeably more at ease now, no longer worried about the idea that he'd ruined his career with his one misstep. Parker was sure that the Bratt family would be pleased.

All in all, it was the perfect meal on the perfect

day and Parker felt a wave of relief wash over him that wasn't the norm. He tried hard to not get upset about anything, but he also was rarely fully relaxed. There was always some crisis sitting in the back of his mind or a worry about one of his clients. Today it was his dad who threatened to make his day less than great. But none of that mattered for now. Parker wouldn't let it.

He and Chloe said their goodbyes to Marcus and made their way back to the guesthouse. The sun had fully set, the night sky deep and dark overhead. Once they stepped into the courtyard, the pool was right before them, looking like sheer heaven. He could imagine how good it would feel to take a dip, the cool water against his skin. Could he convince Chloe to join him? He'd been thinking about it all day. He was willing to risk a no, simply for the chance at a yes.

"Want to go for a swim?" he asked.

"You know I don't have a bathing suit."

"I promise not to look." He knew that was a promise he couldn't really keep, but it at least sounded chivalrous.

"Yeah, right."

"I'll get in naked, too." He swallowed hard, not knowing how she would react to the thing he had not planned on saying. "So neither of us will be at a disadvantage."

"I don't know…"

He shrugged his shoulders. "I can't not get in, Chloe. I'll regret it forever."

"The water does look nice."

"And we've both worked incredibly hard today."

She slid him a look that he couldn't quite decipher. It was part questioning, part mischief. He really hoped she was leaning toward the second. After such a long day, he only wanted to get into that pool with Chloe and see where things went.

This is crazy. Certifiably grade-A nuts. Was she seriously considering getting into the pool with Parker? Naked?

Why yes. Yes, she was.

Because the truth was that she kicked some serious ass today. She'd prepared Marcus perfectly. The interviews she'd arranged for him were right on the money. And he rose to the challenge, just as Parker had said he would. The pool looked unbelievably inviting—a ribbon of calm blue water set against the backdrop of an even deeper blue night sky. Breezes rustled the palm trees. This was exactly what she needed right now—beauty and relaxation. She deserved a dip in that tempting water. And she wouldn't be skinny dipping merely for fun. It was a necessity.

But first she needed a drink. "Can we toast to our successful day first?"

He blew out a short breath of exasperation. "That sounds great. I'll go change into my swimsuit first, though. Just in case you change your mind."

Chloe wondered if he was trying to back out of his promise from moments earlier, but she wasn't going to stress too much about it. "Sounds like a plan." She kicked off her shoes and padded barefoot into the kitchen, grabbing a bottle of white wine from the fridge, a bucket of ice and two stainless steel tumblers. She returned to the pool and sat on the edge, lowering her feet and ankles into the water. The sensation was warm and soft against her skin, made all the more lovely when that heavenly Miami breeze brushed against her face. She finally felt herself uncoil, her breaths became longer and deeper. She didn't want to leave this place. Not anytime soon.

"You aren't going to swim in a skirt and blouse, are you?" Parker's low rumble of a voice came from behind her.

She turned, confronted with the vision of him in his swim trunks, a pair of midnight blue board shorts that hung low around his waist. Now those long easy breaths were short and hard. Every contour of his chest and abs was on full display and Chloe tried not to look, but the truth was that it was impossible. A full day with Parker and she didn't have the energy to keep avoiding the sight of him. She didn't have enough determination to continue squashing down her attraction to him. And here she was giving in to it, looking and drinking him in, but it wasn't like it quenched the thirst. Looking and touching were two distinctly different things. But Parker was not a guy she was supposed to touch. Right?

The injustice ate at her. Why did he have to be a client? Why did they have to have other, messier entanglements, like their family ties? It didn't seem fair. She liked Parker. Even with his arrogant air, his unbridled confidence was contagious. She was drawn to it. Why couldn't they have met in a bar or at a party? He could've been a very fun fling.

"We need to toast." He bent over, picked up the wine bottle and poured himself a glass. "To a job incredibly well done."

"To a job well done." She clinked her glass with his then took a long sip, savoring the cool complexity of the wine as their gazes connected. She endured the rush of attraction between them, the one that seemed to be there every time they made eye contact. It was undeniable for her. Did he feel it, too? Or was that just the way he was? Endlessly magnetic?

He traipsed along the edge of the pool, and Chloe stole her chance to watch him as he walked away, to study the carved contours of his shoulders, the channel of his spine, the hard lines of his waist as it narrowed. When he reached the far end, he dived in, streamlining the entire length under the glassy surface. When he came up for air at the shallow end, his back was to her, water rippling down his skin. He ran his hands through his hair, slicking it back from his face, then turned to her, his eyes bright and full of life.

"You have to get in. The water feels amazing."

"You're right. I should." Chloe swished her feet in the pool. Part of her was scared. She felt like she was perched on the precipice between wise decisions and bad ones. She was tired of being good though. She did it every day, all day long. Week in, week out.

Parker flicked a few drops of water at her, which hit her calves and knees. "Come on. You earned it.

I'm not going to take no for an answer. So here we go." He pulled at the tie on his board shorts and before she really knew what was happening, he was tugging them down his hips and stepping out of them. He balled up the garment, squeezed it and chucked it up on to the pool deck. It landed with a wet thump. The water level was right at his waist and Chloe couldn't see him completely, but she could detect the outline of his trim hips, and simply the knowledge of his nakedness was a turn on. She was far more aware now of the need between her legs. The hunger for Parker.

He waded in deeper, making his way toward her. "I promise that whatever it is that you're hiding under that skirt and blouse, I've seen it all before."

She looked down at him. "I'm absolutely sure of that."

"Actually, I don't mean it that way."

"What do you mean?"

"I've already imagined what you look like without your clothes on. So I've practically seen you naked. At least in my head."

Heat flamed on her cheeks. "You have not."

"Are you kidding me? I imagined it from the first time I saw you get out of that car and I got a glimpse of your thighs." Mischief glinted in his eyes.

A breathless groan left her lips. Why was it so sexy to know he'd thought of her that way? That he'd wanted her bad enough to close his eyes and imagine her without her clothes? "Only once?" She was proud of herself for being so bold and flirtatious. It was so unlike her.

"Fine. More than once." He shrugged it off. "If we're being honest here."

"Oh."

"So, a swim?"

Chloe bit down on her lower lip, allowing herself to make eye contact with him. The connection between them was instantaneous, and just thinking about him fantasizing about her? It only made her want him more. Was there any reason for her to not do this? Of course. But she also saw zero harm in being daring. Of giving in to what she wanted rather than constantly denying her wants. Her needs. She and Parker were all alone in this beautiful house. No one would ever have to know what happened between them. "Yes." She got up from her perch and started for her bedroom. Her heart was pounding in her chest, but it wasn't nerves. It was exhilaration at the prospect of letting loose.

"You'd better be coming back," he called.

"You'd better be quiet," she said in return, flitting across the patio to her room. Inside, she unzipped her skirt and let it fall to the floor as she fumbled with the buttons on her blouse. But as soon as she got that far, something got stuck in her throat. There was part of her that really wanted to be the woman who could boldly walk back out there without a stitch. But that wasn't her. As polished and confident as she worked to be, there were a few well-hidden insecurities inside her. So she kept to her underwear—an exquisite black lace bra and matching panties. She'd ordered the set online, direct from the design house in Paris that Taylor had told her about. It was *not* swimwear. And it wasn't like she was covering up. She was about to get into a pool with a man she was fairly certain she could not resist, Parker, while wearing expensive French lingerie.

And even crazier, he wasn't wearing anything at all.

When she stepped outside, he was waiting for her, standing in the pool with the water just barely to his waist, eyes trained on her bedroom door. He didn't say a thing, leading her to read his face for clues as to what he was thinking. It felt horribly unfair. It played on every insecurity she'd never been able to shake.

But then he smiled and a breathy laugh escaped his lips. "I'd tell you that you're cheating if you didn't look so damn sexy."

She dipped her foot into the warm water and lowered it to the first step. "Is this nuts?"

"Absolutely." He flicked some water at her with the tips of his fingers. "So get wet already."

He was right. She was overthinking this. So she dived under the surface and swam past him, but he caught up to her quickly, his body brushing up against hers as they came up for air. The water was deep enough that she had to hop back and forth on her toes to keep her head above the surface, but he seemed to be flat-footed on the bottom. They both were a bit breathless, so close that she swore she could see his heart beat against his chest.

"Just when I think I have you figured out, Chloe, you surprise me."

"I said I'd get in the pool and here I am."

"True. But you didn't tell me you were going to entice me by showing up in such a seductive outfit. Now I couldn't be any happier that you forgot your swimsuit."

"I'm not as brave as you, Parker. I couldn't just walk out here stark naked."

He inched closer. "I think you are brave."

She wasn't so sure about that, but she was sure of one thing—every second they spent talking was a second wasted. She reached out and grasped his shoulders, and the next thing she knew, his hands were at her rib cage and her feet were no longer on the pool floor. His mouth descended on hers, a kiss that instantly felt naughty and indulgent, as she took what she wanted, her tongue exploring and tasting him. He reached down and grabbed her ass in his hands, squeezing hard and lifting her until his hard length grazed her center and her stomach was against his chest. She wrapped up his shoulders with her arms, pulling him closer to deepen the kiss.

He began walking them toward the shallow end. "I don't care that this is crazy, Parker. I want you." Her voice was a desperate starved-for-breath gasp.

"Good," he growled between their lips. "I want you, too. And I don't think I could live with the disappointment."

Her feet could touch the bottom safely now and she pressed him against the pool wall and kissed him hard, but he met her with a kiss that was so blind with passion she couldn't tell which way was up. All of this being in the water was hot, but she needed him on dry land so she could really see him. Feel him. Touch him. She reared back her head to break their kiss and grabbed his hand to lead him to the stairs.

Step by step the water rolled down her body and she felt Parker's presence right behind her, his hand warm in hers. As soon as he was on the pool deck, he had her in his arms. He walked her over to the spot where there was a double chaise lounge with a thick cushion and lowered her feet to the cement. He tugged down her bra straps until they were at her elbows. The delicate lace cups dropped just far enough for her breasts to leave the confines, and he drank her in like she was the finest champagne, first with his eyes and then with his tongue and lips, which licked and sucked her taut nipples. The heat went straight to her center, which buzzed with need and want. She reached behind her to undo the clasp, tossing aside the garment. How silly that she'd felt like that might protect her. She'd always known she was going to get naked with Parker.

His lips found hers again and she reached down, making first real contact with his steely length. He was rock hard, but his skin seemed to tighten under her touch. He gasped from the pleasure, and she did, too—the pleasure of having him in her hand. He groaned and closed his eyes, a mix of frustration and satisfaction crossing his face when she wrapped her fingers around him firmly, then dragged her hand up, rolling her thumb over the tip, back and forth.

"You're too hot. And I'm going to come if you keep doing that." He kissed her hard then backed up to the chaise, slowly lowering himself to sitting as he kissed his way down her chest, along the flat plane between her breasts and finally her stomach. He leaned back on his elbows, his long body splayed out for her. He was so incredible it was hard to decide where she should look first, so she took in every inch of him as her eyes razed over the landscape of his hard body—sculpted shoulders led to muscled pecs with a tiny patch of hair between them, then a delicious stretch of defined abs and finally the happy trail leading to his magnificent dick.

This is going to be good. As she admired him, she bit down on her lower lip and poked her thumbs into the waistband of her panties, right at her hips, wiggling them down and making a show of tilting her torso forward so he could get the best possible view of her breasts.

She stepped out of them, then straightened, unsure of what came next. They couldn't just stand there and look at each other forever, but there was something so satisfying about that moment of anticipation, where she knew this was going to happen, but they hadn't gotten there yet.

He sat up, then curled his finger in invitation. "Come here."

She smiled and inched closer, then put one knee on the chaise. He wrapped his arms around her waist and lowered her until she was lying on the cushion. He rose to his knees, hovering over her with her legs bracketed by his, then lowered his head, drawing her nipple into his mouth, swirling his tongue perfectly around the tight and sensitive skin. He switched to the other breast then back again, each new contact sending more heat straight to her center, and she raked her hands through his thick wet hair, soaking up every second of the pleasure.

He shifted one knee between her legs, then the other, and she realized his focus had shifted to another area. She was completely bare to him, unquestionably exposed and vulnerable, but she somehow felt both safe and free. He lifted one leg and placed it on his shoulder, then kissed his way along her inner thigh, starting at her knee. Her head rolled back as his lips found her center and his tongue flicked at her clit. He rolled it in artful circles, showing her his talent for pleasing a woman. She wasn't sure how he naturally seemed to know what she liked, but she was so ridiculously thankful for it.

Her head rocked back and forth against the cushion while she felt herself quickly barreling toward her peak. It was intoxicating, especially as the evening breezes brushed against her skin and the warm tropical smells of the Miami night filled her nose. Her mind was a lovely haze of blissful thoughts and earthly pleasures when the tension broke and she felt every muscle in her body go tight and release, pulsing hard. Parker was amazing. And she only wanted more.

* * *

Parker stretched out next to Chloe on the lounge and curled into her, kissing her softly. He was so hard from bringing her to climax that it was difficult to think straight, but he still wanted to be tender with her. From the moment she'd walked out of her room in that sexy lingerie, he knew one thing—she was a seductress who didn't know her own power. She was still playing everything close to the vest. And he only wanted to coax her out of her comfort zone. He took the kiss deeper, coiling his tongue with hers. He didn't need accolades from her—every breathless bit of her desperate kiss told him all he needed to know. He'd rocked her world. And there was more where that came from.

"I should get a condom," he whispered into her ear. "I need to be inside you, Chloe. I need to."

"It depends. I'm on the pill, but it would be good to know you've been checked."

"I had my annual physical a month ago. All clean. All ready for you."

She smiled and kissed him again with those soft lips and velvety tongue that made him absolutely wild. He was losing all sense of time and place, a sensation he never had when he was so eager to get off. Then it was her turn to roll him to his back and hug his hips with her knees. She planted her hands on the cushion on either side of his chest and leaned down into him, kissing him once again. It now felt like true seduction, like she wanted him to know that she could pull him into her orbit if she chose to. And he was so thankful that she'd let him in. But every inch of him pulsed with need and the kiss was so impossibly soft. It was like being tugged back and forth between two worlds…one delighted by anticipation and one burning from it. Her breasts grazed his chest and her nose nudged his cheek as his hands cupped her silky ass and his fingertips dug into her skin. It wasn't enough and yet it was everything. Again, the pull. The tug.

He pulled her hard against his chest, flattening her against his erection, then rolled her to her back. Her red tresses were a messy tumble across the cushion. She wrapped her legs around his waist and he positioned himself at Chloe's entrance. When he drove inside, he realized that as much as he needed her, he wasn't ready for how impossibly good she would feel. They fit perfectly together, like they were made for each other, and that feeling only grew as they quickly fell into a rhythm that felt just right. Deep and hard, while everything about Chloe was soft and luxurious. Warm and welcoming. She hummed her pleasure into his ear, and he answered with a groan, the tension growing in him impossibly fast. She tightened her legs around his hips, her ankles pressed hard against his ass. She scraped her fingernails along the length of his back, a bite of pain that only amplified every sensation. His legs and hips were contracting tighter, winding up like a rubber band about to break. Intensity. Heat. Bliss. It all threatened to engulf him. It might kill him. And he did not care if that was the case.

He changed the angle of his approach, took every stroke deeper, and that was when Chloe's reaction changed, her breaths more fitful, her grip on him that much tighter. She tilted her hips so he could go even deeper, making for another rush that he was unprepared for, overwhelmed by the waves of pleasure that threatened to overtake him. Parker was so close to orgasm that he felt like he was teetering on a knife's edge. It was all a whisper away. But he wasn't ready for it yet. As much as he wanted it, and needed her, he was no dummy. He knew that Chloe was a one-time thing. She would not stick around in his life. This was his chance and he had to take it.

So the second he felt her giving way, he allowed himself to let go as well, and they both hit the peak at the same time. Over and over, the sensations hit him, and each time the edges were a bit softer. Less intense. But that gave way to a feeling of calm he hadn't had in quite some time. As the night breezes rustled the palm trees above them, Parker locked his fingers with Chloe's and brought her hand to his lips. "I no longer think you were dumb for not bringing a bathing suit."

"Why's that?" she asked, rolling to her side and swishing her hand across his stomach.

"Because it totally benefited me."

"I'd say that it benefited both of us." She leaned down and rested her chin on his chest, looking up into his face. "That was hot. Super hot."

He kissed her, but he was already thinking about what came next. More of her. More of them, together.

In his room. On the bed. In the shower. Wherever he could get her. He needed to take what he could from this moment and hold on to it tight. The opportunity wasn't going to present itself to him again. "Darling, you haven't seen hot yet. I will show you hot."

Six

As the uncommonly bright morning sun streamed into the room and Chloe slowly rose into consciousness, she tried not to panic. She was a bit frightened to open her eyes, but she hoped for the best as she prepared to do it. Maybe she was in her own bed. Maybe she wasn't naked. Maybe she hadn't done those things with Parker last night.

Lying on her side, she slowly rolled to her back. The silky sheets glided over her bare skin. *Definitely naked*. With extreme caution, she peeled open one eye, and the vision before her put the rest of the puzzle together. There Parker was, standing at the foot of the bed in his boxer briefs, drinking coffee and looking like a damn underwear model.

"Good morning," he said in that same seductive

voice that had made her want him so badly last night. He wielded it as if it was of little consequence, when in reality it was practically a lethal weapon.

"Morning," she croaked in return, still unable to open her eyes all the way. Or perhaps that was her trying to save herself. If she spent too much time looking at him, he was going to be naked, too, and it wouldn't take a master detective to figure out what would happen next. She'd be arching into him, kissing him with complete abandon and letting him in as deep as she could take him. The thought of it made her shudder with anticipation, but she didn't like what last night had done to her. It had made her weak. She'd lost control. "What time is it?"

"Just after seven. Three hours until Marcus's final interview."

There was a stark reminder of what was wrong— she and Parker were working together. They should not wake up next to each other. "Okay."

"Can I get you some coffee?"

"I'll get it. You don't have to wait on me." Although could she gracefully exit this room right now? She would have to take the entire set of sheets with her if she wanted to be classy about it.

"Suit yourself. I was just trying to be nice."

She sat up in bed, silently willing him to look away or maybe even *go* away. He was nothing short of pure temptation with his sculpted shoulders and long torso. And long legs. And who was she kidding, long *everything*. Memories of last night chased away every other thought. His face burrowed in her neck.

His lips skimming over her breasts. The muscles of his ass flexing against the back of her calves as he rolled his hips and brought her closer to her peak.

"Can I have a bit of privacy, please?" she asked.

"I thought we'd moved beyond that phase of our relationship."

"You're my client." Clutching the bedclothes to her chest, she slid her legs to the side, lowered her feet to the floor, stood and tugged the sheet until it was free. "Last night was a one-time thing. It was a stop on a trip, not a destination. It's time to go back to where we were before. I think we should start by not seeing each other naked anymore."

Parker sipped his coffee nonchalantly. "You act like I expect something from you right now. I can assure you that I expect nothing. We had sex. It's not the end of the world. It's also not the beginning of anything, a sign that we need to establish better rules or anything else that you seem to be constructing in your head, Chloe."

She stared at him. Amazing he could be so nonchalant about it. Like father, like son? Perhaps.

"It was sex," he said yet again. "Nothing else."

She drew a deep breath in through her nose. On the surface, she agreed. And it all made sense, especially coming out of the mouth of Parker Sullivan. He was a playboy. He didn't get attached. And neither did she, which meant everything should have been made good by his assessment of where they were. So why was she taking so little reassurance from his words? Something about it wasn't sitting right with her, but she couldn't quite put her finger on it. "Of course. I know that. I'm just saying that I don't want it to happen again. And the best way to stay on that track is to stop with the nakedness."

"Again with the travel metaphors."

"It works, okay? Time to go home."

"So you don't want to stay one more night? We could have a lot of fun here, just the two of us." He cocked an uncannily expressive eyebrow.

A ripple of heat ran through her so fast she almost passed out. "I really need to get back to the city." *Although that would be incredibly hot and sounds far more tempting than most of the things I have waiting for me back at home.*

"Okay, then. No more fun for us."

"Don't make me into the bad guy here."

He held up his hands in surrender. "Nobody's good or bad. I'm merely stating the obvious."

She took a step toward the door and caught the edge of the sheet with her foot. She bent over and gathered the fabric in her hands, pulling it up until it hit her mid-thigh. Not her most demure look, but it would have to do. "Fine." She breezed past him, but there was something inside her trying to tug her back and make her stay. She ignored it, whatever it was, some poorly timed reflex or a weak impulse. "Marcus's interview is at ten o'clock. He should be done by one. Two at the latest."

"We'll leave for the airport as soon as you want after that. I'll get packed up now," he said when she'd reached the door.

Chloe walked across the breezeway to her room and hopped straight in the shower, trying not to think about the fact that Parker was in the other room. Or the fact that she had so deeply enjoyed having his hands all over her last night. It was a mistake. And she did everything she could to not make mistakes, especially when it came to work. But Parker had made her weak. He had made her want to give in.

She drew in a deep breath, willing the warm spray of the water to wash away her inner conflict. This wasn't the end of the world. No one would ever know that they had slept together. Not Marcus, or her mom, or the world at large. It was a secret. And she had to be thankful for that and simply move on. Back in New York, she could forget about Parker and the brief chapter he'd occupied in her life. She could move on. Like she always did.

Wrapped up in a towel, she padded back into her room and got dressed as quickly as she could, putting on a simple black sheath dress. She was halfway through packing up her things when her phone beeped with a text. She glanced at the screen, mostly to make sure it wasn't anything to do with that morning's interview, but she was nothing but confused by what she saw. It was an image with an odd greenish cast to it, almost like it was taken with night vision technology. It was a woman and a man in a compromising position. *Oh, no.* The woman in that photo was Chloe. And that was not just any man. That was Parker. Someone had been watching them last night? *No, no, no.*

She didn't recognize the number the text had come from and she wasn't sure whether she should reply. But she did know that she had to figure out who was behind this and, even more important, what they wanted.

Who is this? she typed. Her heart raced as she waited for a reply.

I think you know.

Chloe most definitely did *not* know. But she had a sinking feeling it might be related to Marcus and the problems that had brought her down to Miami in the first place. Did this have something to do with Little Black Book? What do you want?

Don't try to stop me.

She twisted her lips. The answer was of little help. It only raised more questions.

From what? How can I stop you if I don't know who you are?

You should know who I am by now.

Are you Little Black Book?

You and your stepbrother need to stop interfering with my mission or I won't be so discreet with the photos.

Chloe dropped her phone on the bed like it was made of fire. "Parker!" Her heart was racing. What in the world was going on?

"What?" He appeared in her doorway. Wrapped in a towel. "What's wrong?" His hair was dripping wet. Droplets of water beaded on his chest. His shoulders were heaving and he was breathing hard. These were not things she needed to see right now.

"Why don't you have any clothes on?"

"Because I was in the shower and you yelled my name. I was worried you were hurt or something had happened."

Even in this moment of crisis, she appreciated his concern for her. "Someone found out about last night."

His eyes narrowed in confusion. "Last night?"

"Yes, Parker. You and me. Having sex. Someone was taking pictures. It has to be Little Black Book. They said we're supposed to stop interfering with their mission. I don't know what that means."

"Show me." He gestured to her phone, which she picked up and unlocked. "Wow. That's us?"

"Someone was spying on us."

"It's grainy as hell, but your ass looks amazing."

"Will you please be serious? This isn't a joke. Do you think it could be Little Black Book?"

"It has to be. I don't know who else it could be. Let's see if they'll answer a call." He pressed the screen a few times and the speakerphone came on—a ringtone followed by three beeps and an automated message. "The number you have reached is no longer in service."

"That was fast."

"They told me to stop trying to stop them, but I'm not. I'm just doing my job."

"Don't worry about it. They're probably just messing with you."

Chloe shook her head. Something told her there was more to it than that. "We can't be around each other anymore, Parker. We're playing with fire. We'll walk Marcus through his interview and part ways."

"That wasn't the threat. They simply told you to stop interfering."

"Yes. I know that. But if my mother finds out that I did that with you, two days after her divorce from your father became final, she would never forgive me." She hadn't felt this uneasy in a very long time. She was used to problems belonging to her clients, not her. She had no objectivity. All she could see was dark clouds ahead. All she felt was panic. "We can't even be seen together. I should probably get on a commercial flight back to New York. Just so we don't risk it."

"Don't be silly. You walk into the main terminal at the airport and there's far more chance someone will spy on you there. We're going straight from the house to the car to my plane. It's fine."

"Why are you acting like this is nothing?"

"Chloe, look at this photo. You're freaking out because you know it's us. But no one else will be able to figure that out. Anyone else is going to think it's just two hot people getting it on."

"This is such a mess. It's a disaster."

"Life is messy. If anyone should know that, it's

you. Just look at our parents. Look at our jobs. Ups and downs, victories and losses and everything in between. Life is a mess."

Chloe understood the point he was trying to make, but that didn't make her any more ready to accept it. She hated it when things were so far out of her control and she was prepared to do anything to restore some sense of order. "I'll fly back with you, but that's the end of the road for us, okay?"

"As long as you'll cut it out with the travel analogies, I'll do whatever you want. I don't have the energy to argue."

Parker turned and quickly ducked back into his room, clutching his towel at his waist. *Dammit.* He was the reason Chloe had gotten that text. He was the one digging. Was he really supposed to call it off now? He didn't want to. Little Black Book served no good in the world. They only wreaked havoc. He didn't want Chloe to get hurt, but he also knew that the best way to get back at Little Black Book was to tear off the mask.

He swiped his phone from the top of the dresser in his room and fired off a text to Jessica. Any update?

Since yesterday? No. Sorry.

He tapped the side of his phone with his finger. She'd said yesterday that she was close to knowing the origin of the diary. In his experience, that meant she was *very* close. Jessica was perfect for her vocation—sneaky and smart. He'd let her get this far, and he trusted her completely. He had to give her the chance to finish the job. Nobody knows?

Nobody.

Great. Thanks.

He blew out a long breath, mulling over the facts he was currently facing. Chloe would kill him if she knew what he was up to. But his fun with Chloe was also over. She was freaked out, and as much as he liked her, he didn't want to battle that. Whatever her hang-ups, he wasn't about to help her work through them. She was determined and she'd been clear about what she wanted from here on out—a return to their former dynamic. If she was okay with one hot night, he should simply accept that, just as he'd done with plenty of other women.

He got dressed, packed up his suitcase and headed to the main house, where he had coffee with Marcus and caught up until Chloe arrived a half hour later. When she walked into the room, the look on her face was a perfect reminder of the state of things. She might be beautiful and beguiling, but she was also all business, and she was done with him.

The next several hours were consumed by Marcus's final interview. He did an exceptional job answering the probing questions, but Parker also knew it was because Chloe had done a flawless job preparing him. As he stood in the background watching,

Parker taped a short segment on his phone, then sent it to Oscar Bratt. Your star quarterback is a natural in front of the camera. Hopefully that would reassure Oscar that Marcus was just as wonderful as originally billed. They'd merely had a little hiccup.

When Parker and Chloe boarded the plane back to New York that afternoon, there should have been a sense of accomplishment in the air. Parker had every reason to be feeling up. Chloe had done an extraordinary job. Marcus had done everything necessary to be back in the good graces of the Bratt family. And when these interviews and magazine spreads were out in the world, things would only improve. Parker's life had regained its equilibrium—the one where he worked hard, played when he had the chance and made piles and piles of money, waiting for the day when it would finally feel like enough.

But as he sat across from Chloe, he couldn't escape the doubts swirling in his head. Their connection last night had been electric, and he'd had a chance this morning to make it into more than a one-night stand. When Chloe woke up and it was clear she was conflicted that they'd had sex, he had *not* seized the opportunity to start a real conversation. He could have sat on the edge of the bed and said that he understood why she was feeling that way. He knew the internal panic that would set in the morning after, when you recognize you'd just shared something incredibly intimate with this other person, but that was as close as you could get. He could have tried to see if there was a way for them to move past it. Instead, he'd taken the easy route, the one that was so entrenched it was like a river carved through a canyon. He'd told her to not make a big deal about it. He'd said it was just sex. It had worked perfectly every other time. Now it just felt off.

Which left him wondering if Chloe truly agreed or if she'd taken the easy way out, too.

"Everything good?" he asked, tossing aside the business magazine he'd flipped through but hadn't actually read.

Chloe looked up from her laptop. "Just getting some work done."

"Busy schedule next week?"

"Yes. How about you?"

"Same." He cleared his throat, confounded by the fact that straying from their professional relationship had managed to make their dynamic *more* business-like. "Seeing your mom when you get back? You said something about Sunday brunch?"

"I am. This is something we've done for years. My mom goes all-out."

Parker wished he had fun traditions like that with his father. Their get-togethers always revolved around work talk. Or money. Or both. To say that Parker felt detached from his family was an under-statement. He was the only child from his dad's first marriage. His mom passed away when he was a teen-ager. He had no bond with his two siblings who came along in his father's later marriages. In fact, Chloe was as close as he'd gotten to anyone associated with his dad in a long time. Or possibly ever.

He sighed, struggling for conversation. He wished he knew what came next with Chloe. It felt as though the door was closing and he wanted to jam his foot in it. But how? "Worried about the photo you got on your phone?"

"Yes." She shut her laptop and set it aside, sitting back in her seat and crossing her legs. "I mean, you made a good point. It was grainy. We knew it was us, but would anyone else? Probably not. So I don't think it lands much of a punch, and I'm guessing Little Black Book knows that. But the whole spying thing and taking photos? They're actively gathering blackmail material. But why?"

Parker swallowed hard. "They obviously know we were in Miami. And they probably know he was doing those interviews. So maybe they're mad that we're trying to counteract the bad publicity?"

She shrugged. "I guess. I still don't like the idea that anyone spied on us. That feels creepy and wrong." She wrapped her arms around her waist and her shoulders shuddered.

"You must encounter situations like this all the time."

"For my clients. Not me. I'm a total homebody. Ninety percent of my life is spent between the office and my apartment. I don't allow myself to get into situations like what happened last night."

Now he wondered if she was talking about romance or the part about being spied on. "Not a lot of hot sex by a pool in Miami?"

She shook her head, but he couldn't ignore the

way the corners of her luscious mouth turned up. She'd had those lips all over him last night and he'd be a fool to not want that again. "No. That does not happen to me often. Or ever."

He took a certain amount of pride at hearing that. "What about your love life, Chloe? Is there one?"

"This sounds like a fishing expedition."

"I'm just curious. Plus, we're stuck on this plane together. We might as well talk about something."

She turned and looked out through the window, seeming deep in thought. "It's pretty anticlimactic. A handful of boyfriends. One broken engagement. Not much really to say about any of it."

"Broken engagement?" Now that really got the wheels in his head turning. He leaned forward, eager to learn more. "You have to spill the beans, Burnett. I want the dirt."

She smiled in a way that made her entire face light up, which in turn sucked the breath right out of Parker. "I like to think of it as a temporary moment of insanity. He asked me to marry him and I said yes, despite my generally terrible image of marriage."

"He must have been a pretty special guy to get you to even consider making that leap." Parker disliked the pang of envy he felt toward this man he didn't even know.

"I think I was caught up in what was going on around me. My friend Alexandra was engaged and planning this totally over-the-top wedding. Her parents were literally spending almost a million bucks on it. It was crazy. And I guess I was just wanting the attention or the excitement of something. This was before I hired Forrest, so work was such a grind and I needed my personal life to be more fulfilling."

"So what happened that you called it off?"

"Alexandra canceled her own wedding."

"With a million dollars on the line?"

Chloe nodded. "Yes. I can't believe you didn't hear about this. It was in all of the New York tabloids. The press had a field day."

"What's your friend's last name? And who was her fiancé?"

"She's Alexandra Gold. She was engaged to Henry Quinn."

Parker slumped back in his chair. "Of course. The Gold–Quinn wedding. I don't read the tabloids at all, but I definitely heard about that. There were terrible headlines."

Chloe sucked in a breath. "Yes. Like I said, the press was brutal to her. Of course, she was an easy target. High society girl calls off million-dollar wedding at the last minute. You don't get much juicier than that."

"I still don't understand how that played into your engagement."

"It was my wake-up call. I had to ask myself what in the heck I was doing getting married. I don't believe in the institution at all. And I certainly didn't want to end up like Alex, with my face splashed all over the pages of the tabloids. So I quietly called it off. My fiancé didn't seem too horribly heartbroken. I think someone else had caught his eye at that point."

"Well, then he's an idiot."

"What are you talking about? You don't believe in marriage either. That's one of the few things we have in common."

"We have a lot more than that in common. We both love our jobs. We both love our parents but think they're ridiculous."

"And we both think marriage is pointless."

Parker worried he might be barking up the wrong tree with pursuing Chloe, but it wasn't like he was thinking of asking her to tie the knot. He simply wanted a little more than the one taste of her. "Can I call you sometime?"

"Sometime? What does that mean?"

"Exactly what it sounds like. Sometime in the future."

She arched both eyebrows at him, seemingly suspicious of his motives. "I don't think that's a great idea."

Parker was glad he'd been vague. He could save some face. "I was talking about work. You know, if another of my clients gets into hot water?"

"Really? Because it sounded like you were asking for permission to make a booty call. You were hoping for a replay of last night."

"What if it was both?"

"I really don't think that's a good idea, especially after that text exchange this morning. And it still brings me back to my original point. My mother would disown me if she knew what happened with you and me. I think we'll both save ourselves a lot of heartache if we chalk this up to what it was."

"Which is what?"

"Exactly what *you* called it. Just sex."

Parker hated himself a little for saying those things. "Right."

"As far as I'm concerned, we both need to move on. Walk in opposite directions as soon as we're back in the city and keep it that way."

Parker wasn't about to accept defeat so easily. "I don't know, Chloe. You and I run in similar circles. We're bound to bump into each other at one point or another."

"We hadn't run into each other before that day I went out to your dad's house on Long Island. I think I can manage to keep my distance."

"Why are you so dead set on closing the door on this? Real life isn't so cut-and-dried, Chloe. It's not all black-and-white. You need to make room for the shades of gray."

"Can't I choose to make my life as cut-and-dried as I want to?"

"Are you saying I can't call you?"

She pulled on her lower lip. He was relentless and she had so little self-control when it came to him. "Let's just say I'll call you."

Seven

Parker's return to New York was not like his usual reentry after a work trip. It held a surprising and unfamiliar sense of emptiness. That feeling started on the plane back from Miami when Chloe had made it clear that she was keeping the ball in her own court. The situation with her mom was too fraught with complications, plus there was the problem of the threat from Little Black Book. Sex with him had not been enough to make her want to bend a few unspoken rules. Which was too bad, because the sex had been fantastic.

He got up early on Saturday morning and went for a long run on his treadmill. He loved the home gym in his apartment, with an expanse of windows that made it feel as though he was taking long strides up above so much of the city, pointed straight at the picturesque Hudson River. But he didn't find himself feeling quite so energized by the view today. It wasn't the Miami guesthouse that was for sure, with its warm sunshine, tropical foliage and beautiful, sexy Chloe in the pool. Just revisiting thoughts of their rendezvous made tension coil tightly in his hips, and that made his legs bind up. Not conducive to a productive run, but all he could think about was kissing her neck and touching her breasts and having her hot breath in his ear. The stunning city vista before him seemed to disappear, replaced by visions of Chloe and her red hair trailing along his chest as she kissed her way down his stomach…

You're tormenting yourself.

He hit the stop button on the treadmill and hopped off, grabbing a towel to wipe the sweat from his face. Why was he off in fantasy land? He was not a guy with his head in the clouds and he also wasn't anywhere close to this desperate. And even if he was, it was in his power to change that. There were plenty of women's numbers on his phone. All he needed to do was make a call or two, deliver an enticing invitation and get his mind off the one woman who he apparently couldn't have. And his Saturday would not have to be a complete waste.

He grabbed his phone, but just as he was about to scroll through his contacts, the screen lit up with a video call from his dad. He pressed the green button, grabbed his water bottle and started for the kitchen. "Hey, Dad. What's up?"

"I see you're back from Miami." His dad's formidable face filled the screen—stern blue-gray eyes and a jawline that was all business. His father was aging well and Parker hoped for the same, especially the full head of silver hair his dad had.

"I am."

"And do you feel you were successful in shutting down this gambling story?"

Parker nodded and took a seat on one of the barstools at his kitchen island. "Definitely. Once these articles run, the world can see that Marcus is not this one mistake. He's a smart, talented and handsome young man who owns an amazing Miami mansion and is in ridiculously good shape."

"I've been meaning to ask, who did you hire to do Marcus's publicity? Good crisis PR is hard to come by."

Parker hadn't banked on this question. His father rarely probed for details. He was primarily a guy who wanted to know that things were taken care of, and that was usually the end of the conversation. "Actually, this is a funny situation. I think you'll get a kick out of this." He swallowed hard, hoping that would prove to be true. "I hired Chloe Burnett."

For a moment, Parker's dad did nothing but stare into the camera on his phone. Slowly, a smile started to curl the corners of his mouth. "You're kidding."

"I'm not. I finally met her the day that she came out to the house on Long Island to get her mother's things. We chatted for a few minutes about work, she told me what she does and that was that. But then the

Marcus story broke a few hours later. She impressed me, so I called her up and the rest is history." Parker was having a hard time containing his own smile as the flashbacks to Miami started again.

"And you were pleased with the job she did?"

"One hundred percent."

"Good to know."

"This isn't a problem for you, is it? I mean, considering that you just got divorced from her mom?"

"Actually, it might help me. You hiring Chloe might make Eliza hate me a little less. Things were not great at the end there." His dad sighed and looked off for a moment. "Then again, they never are when a marriage is falling apart."

"Are you doing okay with everything?"

His dad dismissed the question with a tut. "Yes. It's better this way. Believe me."

Parker had very few heart-to-heart conversations with his dad, but he couldn't help but feel like this might be a good time to try. As much as he disliked his father's habits in his personal life, it tore him up to see him ride this roller coaster of romantic highs and lows. "I know you don't like to talk about this, but maybe it's a good idea for you to take a break from relationships for a while."

"You're giving *me* advice about my love life?"

"Don't think of it as advice so much as a suggestion from your well-meaning son."

"Parker, you're thirty-four and I couldn't tell you the last time I met someone you were dating. From where I sit, you shuffle women in and out of your life like they're nothing. I'm not sure that your approach is a good one either. At least I'm willing to commit."

Parker didn't see it that way. At all. "Marrying every woman you've slept with more than twice isn't particularly respectful either, is it? You promise them the world and then you get bored." He stopped himself from saying what he really wanted to get off his chest, that his father ultimately treated his mother that way, even when she was sick. Parker braced for an outburst from his father.

His dad's anger never came. Instead, he shrugged. "Maybe that is what I do. Life is messy, Parker. I've told you that hundreds of times."

Those were the exact words Parker had said to Chloe on the plane back from Miami. No wonder she hadn't been particularly receptive to the idea. Yes, life was messy, but some people were agents of chaos in their own lives and couldn't see it. Parker had long thought his dad was one of those people. And now that the man was in his early sixties, Parker couldn't see ever persuading him to change. "I don't want to argue, Dad. You do what's best for you. But maybe stay away from Vegas if you can."

"Don't worry. I plan to play the field for at least a little while."

"Are you bringing anyone to the hospital fundraiser on Friday?"

"I've decided not to go."

"But we always go together. It's tradition."

"All they really want from me is a check. They'll get their money."

Parker couldn't believe what his dad was saying. They'd attended the fundraiser for the cancer wing at the hospital since Parker was a teenager, the year after Parker's mom passed away. "It still says something for you to be there."

"It's time for you to carry that torch. That's the way your mom would have wanted it anyway."

Parker wasn't a sentimental guy and he tried not to think about his mom too much—losing her had been one of the most difficult things he'd ever experienced. "Do you think about her?"

"She creeps into my thoughts most days."

Parker sighed. "Yeah. Me too."

"But I don't like to get too wrapped up in it, either. I loved your mother, but we did not have a perfect marriage. I don't want to put her on a pedestal she might not wish to be on."

"Do you think I do that?"

"You're her son. It's your job to not only put her on the pedestal, but to keep her there. Which is why I think it's important that you're the family representative at that fundraiser."

"Oh, I'm definitely going. A few of my clients will be there."

"All the more reason for you to go. But don't let the whole night be about work. There's more to life than that."

Parker nodded, taking in his father's words. He hadn't counted on so much life advice. "Thanks, Dad. I appreciate it."

"Thank you for straightening things out with Oscar Bratt."

"Yeah. Of course."

"I'd better get going. I'm heading out for a round of golf in a few minutes."

"Have fun." Parker said goodbye to his father and ended the call. The phone was still in his hand and the things his dad had said were echoing in his head...*don't let the whole night be about work*. Perhaps if he invited Chloe to the fundraiser, she would see that he really wasn't the guy she thought he was.

Of course, she'd said that *she* would call *him*. That made this tricky. And messy.

Then again, he liked messy.

And if he spent any more time thinking about it, he'd find a dozen reasons to talk himself out of it— why put yourself out there? Why risk the rejection? Why not call a woman who'd be eager to say yes? The answer was that he only wanted Chloe. So he pulled up her number and pressed the green button. With every ring, his confidence waned a bit more. Was she staring at his name on the caller ID and deciding whether she wanted to speak to him? That was a real possibility.

Eventually, the ringing stopped. "You've reached Chloe Burnett. Leave a message." For an instant, he considered hanging up and moving on. He had other options. There were other women he could invite to the fundraiser.

But Chloe was the one occupying his thoughts. He couldn't shake her. So he took a deep breath and went for it. "Hey, Chloe. It's Parker. I hope you're doing well." He got up and walked over to the window, his mind racing for the right way to ask the question. "I know you said that you would call me, but this couldn't wait. I have to go to a fundraiser for the cancer hospital Friday night and my dad usually goes, but he's bowing out this year. I was hoping you might come with me. I guess I just felt like things were cut very short at the end of our trip. I'd like to be able to spend a little more time with you. If you're up for it." He drew in a deep breath, feeling as though he might have dug himself a very deep hole. "So, yeah. Call me if you're interested."

Chloe was late for brunch at her mom's. She anxiously looked out the car window as Liam breezed north on Madison Avenue to the Upper East Side, having little trouble navigating the city streets on a Sunday morning. She was almost never behind schedule. She was a stickler for punctuality. But ever since Parker had left her that message yesterday, she'd been off-kilter. She thought she'd closed the door on any involvement with him, but apparently he wasn't willing to take no for an answer. The thing that was really throwing her off was the event he'd invited her to. A hospital fundraiser? That was *not* a date. Nor was it a recipe for seduction. So maybe he merely didn't want to go alone. She wasn't sure what he was after. She also wasn't sure whether she wanted to provide whatever it might be.

She arrived at her mother's apartment building on

Madison at 89th St., just a block from Central Park, a few minutes after eleven o'clock. She rushed inside when the doorman let her in, only to find Alex and Taylor waiting near the elevator.

"You're late," Taylor said, tucking one side of her blond bob behind her ear. She was dressed in black from head to toe, which anyone else might find somber attire for Sunday brunch, but it was pretty normal for her.

"We figured we should wait and go up with you," Alexandra said, smiling sweetly. She was her usual gorgeous self, in a fun and feminine deep teal dress that really brought out her warm brown eyes. Her dark hair was up in a high ponytail, highlighting her perfect cheekbones.

Chloe hugged both of her friends then pressed the button for the elevator. "Thanks for coming on short notice. It'll make my mom happy. She's still nursing her wounds from the divorce."

"It probably doesn't help that you took a job with her ex-husband's son," Taylor said.

Chloe should have known better than to tell Taylor about that little detail. "Please don't say anything about it in front of my mom. She doesn't know and I intend to keep it that way."

The elevator dinged and the three stepped on board.

"Why do you guys tell me this stuff with no warning?" Alex asked. "You know I'm not good at keeping secrets."

"Look, here's the situation. I took a quick job from

Parker Sullivan, but it was mostly to prove to him that what I do is actually a valuable service." Chloe cleared her throat, knowing she was already sounding defensive. "It wasn't a big deal. Just a night in Miami together." As soon as those last words were out of her mouth, she regretted sharing that information. Her voice had reached a pitch that she knew her friends would pick up on.

Alex and Taylor exchanged knowing looks, then Taylor slammed the stop button on the elevator. "Hold on one second. Something happened in Miami, didn't it? With Parker."

Chloe was panicked. "Taylor. You can't do that. They'll call building security." She reset the emergency button and the elevator lurched as it resumed its trip upstairs.

"I want details, Chloe. Dirty, filthy details," Taylor said.

The door slid open to Chloe's mother's floor. "How do you even know there are any details?" Chloe whispered, quietly stepping into the grand foyer.

"I can tell," Taylor said.

"She can tell." Alex nodded eagerly as if this all made perfect sense.

"I can't believe you slept with your stepbrother," Taylor said under her breath.

"Former. *Former* stepbrother." Chloe shook her head. "You two are unbelievable."

"Girls? Is that you?" Chloe's mom's voice came from somewhere off in the expanse of the apartment.

Funny that she still referred to them as girls, even though they were in their thirties.

"It's us, Mom. We'll be right there," Chloe called back. "Can we please just have brunch and not talk about this?" she asked Alex and Taylor.

Taylor unleashed a devilish smile. "You always tell us everything eventually. I'll get it out of you one way or another."

"If there was hot sex involved, I definitely want to know," Alex added. "I have no sex life. I need to live vicariously through someone."

Chloe's face flamed so hot it was like she'd stuck her head in a lava flow. The worst part was that she was sure the heat had turned her cheeks bright pink.

"So there *was* hot sex." It wasn't a question from Taylor. She was making an assertion.

Chloe pointed at Taylor, then Alex. "Both of you. Shush."

"You can tell us in the elevator on the way down," Alex said.

"Girls! Mimosas are waiting," Chloe's mom announced in a singsong from the other room.

The three friends strode down the long central hall past two well-appointed guest bedrooms and her mother's showplace of an office, then into the main living space—a great room with the gourmet kitchen her mother rarely used on one side and casual seating on the other. Most of the apartment was tastefully decorated in white and cream with the occasional bit of gray. Her mother's other homes—the historic family mansion in the Hamptons, the terrace house in London, the lodge in Aspen and the seaside estate in Hawaii weren't all so neutral. But the Madison Avenue apartment was home base, and a place for her mom to reset when she was newly single, thus the calming color scheme.

"I'm so glad you three are here!" Chloe's mom exclaimed, throwing her hands up in the air then rushing over to wrap Chloe up in a quick but warm embrace. Chloe noticed that her mom felt a bit skinny, but that was normal for her in the wake of a breakup.

"Hi, Mom. It's so good to see you." Chloe inhaled the enticing aroma of something delicious baking in the oven.

"We wouldn't miss this for the world, Ms. B.," Alex said, eagerly taking her own hug.

Taylor followed. "Thanks for having us."

"It's long overdue. I'm sure there's a lot we need to catch up on." Chloe's mom began to unwrap a platter of artfully arranged fruit, which had undoubtedly been assembled by her personal chef. Her mom didn't cook. But she did present other people's culinary efforts with flair. Per usual, her mom was very put together, in dark jeans and a white sweater with deep crimson lipstick. Her red hair—a near match for Chloe's—tumbled past her shoulders. "I'll just finish getting out the food for everyone. Taylor, if you could pour the mimosas that would be great."

Taylor filled four glasses, then pulled a barstool up to the center island and took a sip of her drink. "Did you hear Chloe went to Miami?"

Chloe shot her friend a look. "Mom knows. She and I talked the morning I left."

"I see you didn't have any time in the sun while you were there. You've still got that early spring pale," her mom said, slipping on a pair of oven mitts just as the kitchen timer went off.

"I was only there for a short time," Chloe replied.

"Yep. Just a quickie," Taylor added.

Chloe made a mental note to threaten Taylor with the revocation of her brunch privileges if she was going to misbehave this way.

"Tell me the latest, Taylor. You too, Alexandra," her mom said as she pulled a quiche from the oven.

Taylor launched into what Chloe already knew, that she was unhappy with her job as an events planner, and still doing everything to avoid men. Alex was the other side of the spectrum—she adored her job as a high-end floral designer, and was eager to have a real return to dating, but her love life wasn't as simple as that. Since she'd canceled her million-dollar wedding and had her face splashed all over the pages of the tabloids, she'd found men to be gun-shy about being with her.

"So, I met a man," Chloe's mom said with an unmistakable purr in her voice.

"Mom. I was gone for two days. Are you serious right now? Don't you think you should take a break?"

Her mother laughed—a sure sign that she was already head over heels. "There's no dictating love, darling."

Chloe was even more dismayed now. Her mom

had used the "L" word. "And you just went through a nasty divorce."

"Every divorce is nasty. Mine is no different. I think it's time to move on."

Chloe felt like she had whiplash from her mother's ever-changing moods—one minute she was miserable and vindictive, the next minute she was sunny and willing to let things go. "I think you need to spend some time figuring out what you want." Chloe tried to ignore the fact that she, too, needed to figure out what the hell she wanted. Her mind kept flying back to Parker. It felt like they had unfinished business. Or she at least wanted to get him out of her system. But she also had this sense that there was something else there. Something bubbling under the surface.

"What I want is to have fun, and you should try the same. It might help you loosen up a bit. You take everything so seriously." Her mom slugged back her mimosa. "Now who's ready to eat?"

The four women sat in the informal dining area off the kitchen and Chloe tried to focus on having fun with her friends and spending quality time with her mom. These were the most important people in her life, period, and she wanted to soak up all of that goodness. But she was worried about her mother, and about what she might do. Was there another marriage on the horizon? Chloe hoped to hell not.

After much discussion of careers and men, along with several mimosas and a whole lot of food, things began to wind down. Cleanup was quick with four of them there, and it was soon time to go. Alex and Taylor said their goodbyes first, leaving the final farewell to Chloe. She waited until her friends had left the room before she expressed her concern.

"Mom." Chloe took both her mother's hands in hers and peered into her soft brown eyes. Despite her mother's many flaws, the love Chloe felt for her went deep. It physically pained Chloe whenever her mom was unhappy. "I hope you know that all I want for you is to be happy. That's sincerely all I want."

Her mom nodded. "I appreciate that, darling. I really do. I know you think I'm always getting in over my head, but this time is different. I'm having fun with my new guy. That's all it is. If nothing else, he sure is helping me forget George. Everything that was bothering me about that split is suddenly fading into the background. It's like it never happened."

"Well, there's definitely something to be said for that."

"What about you?" she asked.

"What do you mean?"

"Your love life. You never tell me a peep. I worry that you work too hard. It would be nice if you settled down at some point. Maybe made me a grandparent someday? That would be wonderful."

Chloe was so far from marriage and motherhood that she wasn't residing in the same hemisphere. "There's one guy, but I'm not sure you'd like him. And it's just a fling. Or maybe even less than a fling."

"I like anyone you like. Without question. And as for flings, it can turn into more. It can also just be fun, and there's absolutely nothing wrong with that. I've learned that, as a woman, you need to learn to take what you want. Don't sit back and worry about what the rest of the world will say."

That certainly gave Chloe a lot to think about. "Okay, Mom. I should get going, but thank you for hosting today. It was really nice for everyone to get together."

"Any time. I loved it." Her mom gave her one more hug, then walked her to the foyer, waving goodbye to Alex, Taylor and Chloe as the elevator door slid closed.

"Spill it, Chloe," Taylor immediately said.

Chloe had thought about it and decided this was info best kept to herself. Instead of answering, she held her fingers to her lips, turned an imaginary key and tossed it over her shoulder. "Sorry. I'm not going to kiss and tell."

"Tequila," Taylor said. "We need to get some serious liquor in you. Then you'll tell us everything."

The elevator dinged and they strolled out into the lobby. "Chloe doesn't have to tell us a thing if she doesn't want to," Alex said once they were out on the street.

"Whose side are you on, anyway?" Taylor asked.

"The side of my friends," Alex said. "Which means that I respect your wishes. No matter what."

A black SUV pulled up to the curb. "That's me. I'll see you both soon," Taylor said, kissing both Chloe and Alex on the cheek.

Alex laughed as Taylor's driver sped off. "She's such a crazy woman. But I love her for it."

"Yeah. Me too," Chloe said. "So what do you have going on this week?" she asked while they both waited for their drivers to pick them up.

"I have to go to this hospital fundraiser that I did the flowers for. I really, really don't want to go. I don't have a date, and I hate going to those things by myself." It was as if a light bulb had gone off and her eyes grew larger. "Oh, my God. Do you want to come with me?"

Given the earlier invite from Parker, this was certainly an interesting turn of events. "Hospital fundraiser?"

"Yep. Friday night. At the Waldorf. It's a great excuse to wear a fancy dress and there's an open bar." Alex tugged on her hand. "Come on. You know you want to. Plus, you and I never get to spend any time together, just the two of us. It'll be fun."

This might be the perfect solution to Chloe's Parker predicament. She didn't have to accept his invitation, but she could still see him. It would give her a chance to test the waters. Dip her toe in one last time and see if perhaps she'd simply been under the spell of Parker in Miami the first time. There was a chance that Parker in Manhattan might not prove quite as tempting. "I'd love to go. But full disclosure, the guy from Miami is going to be there."

"Parker Sullivan?"

"Yes."

"How do you know he'll be there?"

"Because he invited me to the event and I haven't given him an answer yet."

Alex narrowed her sights on Chloe. "I like it. You can see him without actually letting him know you're interested. Very clever."

Chloe loved how well her friends knew her. "Exactly."

Alex's driver approached the curb and Chloe could see that Liam was pulling up right behind him. "So? Friday? It's a date?" Alex asked.

"Yes." Chloe nodded. "I look forward to it." She climbed into the car and pulled out her phone, staring at it for a few minutes before finally calling Parker.

"Hey," he said when he answered.

She wasn't quite prepared for what his voice did to her. It made her insides turn to liquid. Thoughts of Miami zipped through her head—bare skin and warm tropical breezes and kisses that could seriously make her forget her own name. "Hey, yourself."

"I take it you got my message?"

"I did."

"And?"

Chloe wasn't quite sure how to word this, since she still didn't know if the invitation he'd extended was a date. "Turns out that my friend Alexandra is going, too. She and I don't get to see each other very often, so I was thinking that I'll go with her and see you there?"

A few long moments of silence played out on the other end of the line. She had to wonder what he was thinking. Was he disappointed? Rejected? Or maybe

something far less consequential, like distracted?
"Sure thing. That sounds great. I hope you'll let me
buy you a drink."

"Alex said there's an open bar."

Parker laughed, which sent a flutter through her.
"Oh, right. That was stupid of me to say. How about
this? I'll wait on you. I'll bring you whatever you
want."

"Are we still talking about a drink?"

"Maybe. Or maybe other things. I haven't decided
yet."

Chloe couldn't fight the smile breaking across her
face. "Anything I want?"

"Absolutely anything."

Eight

Parker was annoyed Chloe hadn't truly accepted his invitation. She'd said yes in the most roundabout noncommittal way. But he also felt challenged, and that got his blood pumping at the thought of what it might take to get her to stop being so damn cautious about him. She didn't seem like a woman who would enjoy a game of cat and mouse. She was all about black-and-white. Cut-and-dried. Yes or no. Or so he'd thought.

There was another factor at play here. She might still be nervous about Little Black Book leaking those blurry photos. If the topic came up, Parker would have to point out that here they were nearly a week later, and Little Black Book had not made good on its threat.

Sitting in the back of the limo on the way to the hotel, he received a text from Jessica, his investigator. I found the origin of the diary.

Speak of the devil. Parker could hardly dial the phone to call Jessica fast enough.

"That was quick," she said when she answered.

"I'm impatient. And ridiculously curious about who is behind this." Parker didn't let many things get to him, but he couldn't help it when it came to Little Black Book. He checked the social media account every morning and every night before he went to bed. He took note of the way their follower numbers continued to steadily climb. He studied the array of rich and powerful people who came into their crosshairs. There were politicians and Hollywood A-listers, Wall Street bigwigs and a wide variety of American royalty. Were they really considering Parker and Chloe for a future target? Or had it all been a bluff?

He suspected it was the latter, but it had struck a little too close to home the day before when the dad of one of Parker's college friends became a target. He was a bank president and had apparently loaned large sums of money to an investment guru involved in a pyramid scheme. He'd reportedly tried to hide the loans by moving the debt to the family's shell companies, but this rumor was starting to catch up with him, especially since there was chatter that his own dad had done something similar in the 1970s. It wasn't that Parker didn't want bad people held accountable for their misdeeds. He did. It was more that it was a little too easy for Little Black Book to hide behind the mask and shoot arrows, never having to face any real scrutiny.

"After some handwriting analysis, I feel strongly that the diary belonged to Simone Astley, a socialite from Connecticut," Jessica said. "From everything I've been able to learn, she had freakishly good hearing and her family was very connected. She spent years eavesdropping and picking up on other people's secrets and keeping track of everything she became privy to."

It was an intriguing idea, but Parker found this answer less than satisfying. "But she's dead, isn't she?"

"Yes."

"So it's her diary, but no one knows who actually has it?"

"No one I've spoken to knows."

"I still don't get it. They're breaking current scandals, then dredging up old secrets, too. What's that all about?"

"Hard to say. I'm just telling you what I've learned so far. She had no siblings and never had kids, so her estate is just sitting up in Connecticut. The property was left to the local historical society, but it doesn't appear they've done anything with it. Anyone could have gotten their hands on her diary. Anyone."

"Can you go up there and scope it out?"

"Do you really want to spend your money on this? Marcus and his family don't seem to be a target anymore."

Jessica had a point, but Parker still wasn't willing to let it go. Little Black Book had been spying on Chloe and him in Miami. He might not be losing sleep over it, but he wasn't about to ignore that completely. "Just head up there for a day. If you don't find anything, we'll drop it."

"It'll have to be next week or maybe the week after if that's okay. My schedule is crazy."

"Too many demanding clients insisting you cater to their every whim?"

She laughed. "You might say that. I'll do what I can, okay?"

"Thanks, Jess."

"You're welcome."

Parker said goodbye and hung up just as his driver, Benny, was pulling up to the Waldorf hotel. There were at least six or seven cars ahead of them, and Parker didn't particularly want to wait. "You can let me out here."

"You sure, Mr. Sullivan? I'm not really doing my job if I don't drop you at the door."

Parker reached for the door handle. "You're just going to get stuck in that long line of limos anyway. Save yourself the headache."

"Whatever you say, sir. Text me when you're ready to be picked up."

"Will do." Parker exited the car and strode along the sidewalk, then turned up the walk to the hotel. It felt strange to be here without his dad. They'd attended this event together many times. Apparently, it was time to turn the page on that. He made his way inside, waving to a few familiar faces, but moving undeterred across the luxe lobby to the escalator leading up to the second-floor ballroom. He couldn't help but be on high alert for Chloe, wondering what it would be like to see her again. Would there be more cat and mouse? He enjoyed a good game of pursuit every now and then, but only when there was an end in sight.

He walked up to the check-in table. The woman with the guest list immediately knew who he was, handing over his name tag before he could remind her. "Here you go, Mr. Sullivan. Enjoy yourself."

"Will do." He took one more quick survey of the area outside the ballroom. No sign of Chloe, so he headed inside. Right away, he spotted the first of his two clients attending—women's professional basketball player Danisha Porter. Danisha had brought her husband and sister. After a short conversation and another casual search for Chloe, Parker tracked down his second client—hockey great Andrei Eichen. Like Parker, both of his clients had lost someone they loved to cancer, and felt the need to donate their time to the cause, lifting patients' spirits by visiting them in the hospital while undergoing treatments. Parker knew from experience that it was a very fulfilling thing to do. Every time he'd tagged along, which was more often than not, he always left feeling a little better about his line of work. On the surface, it was just sports and big paychecks. But he'd managed to bring deeper meaning to it. At least for himself.

Unfortunately, there was still no sign of Chloe and the ballroom was quickly filling up to capacity with hundreds of well-dressed guests. It was great to see such a fantastic turnout. That meant more money raised, but it also made it that much more difficult to track down Chloe. And Parker could admit that was all he really cared about right now.

And then, like a dream, she stepped into his vision. She was wearing an off-the-shoulder icy blue satin dress with a very pleasing neckline. Her flame-red hair fell around her face in rolling waves. Even with the considerable cache of hot memories from their time in Miami, Parker could hardly believe he'd managed to survive the week since they'd returned. One look at her and his entire body was on fire. It was game on for cat and mouse, and he wasn't about to lose. Winning could only involve seeing her dress on the foyer floor in his apartment. Or maybe thrown across the back seat of his limo. He had to have her again.

If he was lucky, again and again.

He wanted to play it cool, but he wasn't going to play the fool. He wound his way through the crowd to get to her. When he was about halfway there, their eyes connected, and he relished the jolt of electricity he had to endure when the corners of her luscious mouth turned up into a smile. Every step closer brought more anticipation. He wanted to touch her. Smell her. Kiss her. A few feet away and he swore her beguiling scent filled his nose. He wanted to nestle his face in her curviest spots. He wanted to put his mouth all over her, wanted to taste her skin. "You're here," he said, reaching for her elbow and planting a kiss on her cheek. His eyes were drawn to the sumptuous curves of her cleavage, and his hands twitched with recognition of what it was like to have her velvety breasts in his hands.

"Of course I am. I told you I would be." She slid him a sly grin. "You weren't actually worried about it, were you?"

"Never. I don't worry. I think you know that by now."

"Oh, right. Remind me to get a lesson in patience from you at some point." Her eyes flashed with a sexy glimmer.

"Not worrying isn't the same as being patient. I assure you that when I want something, I don't like to wait."

"Good to know." Chloe turned as a curvy brunette woman walked up to them. "Parker, meet Alexandra. Alexandra, this is Parker," Chloe said, carefully studying them as they shook hands.

Parker was intrigued by Alexandra, but mostly because it helped him put Chloe in context. Alex was beautiful, but she was also very quiet. Almost meek. This was the woman Chloe had been trying to keep up with when she got engaged? Parker didn't totally get it. "It's really nice to meet you, Alexandra. I've heard a lot about you."

Alexandra blushed. "Please. Call me Alex. And don't believe everything you've heard."

"Oh. I didn't mean the tabloid stuff. Just the things that Chloe told me about."

"You'd have to be living under a rock to not know about the tabloids," Alex said.

Chloe stepped closer to Parker and clutched his arm, which he loved. "Actually, I had to remind him about the story. He didn't really remember it."

"Seriously?" Alex asked, seeming shocked.

"Seriously," Parker answered. He could appreciate that she must be feeling self-conscious about having been splashed all over the front page of several gossip rags. "You seem like you've emerged unscathed. So that's good."

Alex shrugged. "I'm trying."

Just then, one of the women from the hospital tapped Parker's shoulder. "Mr. Sullivan, can I have a quick chat with you? In private?"

Parker was both confused and disappointed. He'd finally found Chloe and now duty called. "Is there something wrong?"

"Just something I'm hoping you can help me with."

He turned to Chloe, desperate for her to know that as soon as he finished whatever this was about to be, the rest of his night was all for her. "Don't go anywhere, okay? I'll be right back in a few minutes."

Chloe smiled wide. "Don't worry. I'll stay put."

"Good. I want you right where I can find you."

Chloe didn't want to admit how much she hated seeing Parker walk away from her, but she did. Especially when he was looking perfect in a classic black tux *and* was accompanied by such a beautiful woman. "I wonder what that was all about," she said to Alex.

"Not sure. Is Parker involved in tonight's event?"

Chloe shrugged. "I don't know. I thought this was just a fundraiser he was attending, like any other event. He never said a peep about it before he invited me the other day."

"Do you want to tell me what happened in Miami? You don't have to if you don't want to."

Chloe knew her cheeks were turning bright red. "Things went to a place I wasn't exactly expecting. Let's put it that way."

"Don't worry. I get what you mean. And I don't need the full breadth of details like Taylor does."

"Thank you. I appreciate that."

"Do you think you two could be an item?"

Chloe's immediate reaction was to wave off the very idea. It still didn't make sense to her, even though she liked Parker a lot. "No. The history between his dad and my mom is more than enough reason to stay away from each other. And we're both staunchly opposed to commitment."

"He might feel like that, but do you? Really? I mean, you did get engaged to Kurt."

"That was a mistake. He asked and part of me thought that it wasn't such a terrible idea."

"I hate to break it to you, but I think that part of you is still in there."

Chloe stifled a sigh. "Maybe. I don't know. Kurt was a mistake, though. Surely you can appreciate that sometimes we make poor choices when it comes to men."

"Look, we're not talking about me. And I've heard

this story from you one hundred times, Chloe. It's getting old. You're not your mom. I hope you know that. And just because she's had a bumpy road in that department doesn't mean you'll meet the same fate."

"I'm amazed you can be optimistic about relationships at all."

"If I don't stay positive, I'll drown in a sea of my own tears."

Perhaps that was true for Alex, but Chloe remained unconvinced. "Doesn't matter. I'm in zero rush to get serious again. Zero." She had to wonder if coming here tonight had been a bad idea. She didn't like big events like this. If she was going to meet people and shake hands, she preferred to do it in the comfort of her own office, preferably when the person she didn't know was desperate for her services. It made for a much better dynamic. And then there was the issue of Parker. What did he want from her? What did she want from him?

"Oh, my God," Alexandra said, grabbing Chloe's arm. "Ryder Carson is here."

"Oh, cool. You should go say hi." Ryder was Alex's brother's best friend, but Alex had known him for years.

"Unfortunately, it's not quite as simple as that."

"Why?"

"I kissed him. On New Year's Eve."

"Wait. What? The party we were all at? Together?" Chloe, Alex and Taylor had attended a big New Year's party hosted by Alex's brother. "You never said a thing about that. How did I miss that?"

Chloe certainly hadn't been busy kissing anyone else. She'd gone home with a headache from too much champagne and a distinct lack of guys worth kissing.

"You know I've always had a thing for him. Like a big thing." Alex bit down on her lip. "And we were standing near each other when the ball dropped and I don't know, I guess I just lost my head for a minute. So I kissed him."

"How did he react?"

"He was super into it for about two seconds and then I think he realized that my brother was in the same room. He said he had to go get a drink of water, but I never saw him again. He took off."

"Your brother can be pretty intimidating. And he's also very protective of you. I'm not surprised."

"Maybe he was feeling like he'd violated the bro code. You know, where guys won't date their friends' sisters or their exes for that matter."

"And you haven't spoken to him since?"

Alex shook her head, but she had this wistful look in her eye as she watched Ryder across the room. "I haven't."

"Do you want to talk to him?"

"Sorta. I mean, I'm worried he's going to tell me to go away or something, too."

Chloe grabbed two glasses of champagne from a waiter who strolled past them. "Here. Take this for strength. A sip or two, then go say hello and see what happens. Worst-case scenario, he's weird about it, but like most guys, he'll probably just ignore the elephant in the room."

"Maybe." Alex seemed unconvinced.

Just then, Chloe spotted Parker again on the other side of the room. He was still chatting with the woman from earlier, but he was looking right at Chloe. Rather than waving, he cocked an eyebrow at her. It made her body temperature spike. "Go talk to Ryder. I'm going to talk to Parker. We'll meet up later, okay?"

"Sounds good."

Chloe began weaving past people so she could talk to Parker. All this conversation about people not knowing where they stand, it was all starting to get to her. She wanted to know what tonight was about. She wanted to know what in the hell Parker wanted from her. Unfortunately, when she reached him, he was still chatting with his admittedly beautiful friend. Chloe tried not to bristle at the jealousy creeping up inside her, but it was difficult to ignore. It registered deep, a dull ache that showed no sign of going away. If this woman was interested in Parker and he felt the same way, Chloe was going to need a while to get over that.

"Chloe, come here." Parker waved her closer. "I want you to meet Jillian." He turned to the woman. "Jillian, this is Chloe. Chloe is my date this evening."

Date? That made Chloe's ears perk up, but she wasn't going to ask for clarification in front of Jillian. Instead, she reached out for a handshake. "Nice to meet you. How do you two know each other?"

"Parker's the hospital's star volunteer. We work together all the time," Jillian said.

"Really?" Chloe asked, hoping she didn't sound too horribly astonished, even though she was.

"Did he not tell you about that?" Jillian asked.

Chloe shook her head. "No. He did not."

Jillian patted him on the shoulder. "So modest. He's the absolute best. He not only raises millions of dollars for us every year, he gets his clients involved, too. They attend fundraising events like tonight, and Parker also arranges for his star athletes to visit our patients, in their homes and at the hospital. It's a huge hit with everyone, even the staff. It's such a hard situation for everyone, but the visits make it so much better. It really boosts morale."

Chloe felt her jaw drop, but she quickly rectified the situation by speaking. "Amazing." *As in truly.* What the hell? This was not the Parker she thought she knew—Mr. Playboy was not the guy who went the extra mile for charity. Even more perplexing, that guy would at least brag about it. But not Parker.

"I should get going. It was nice to meet you, Chloe." Jillian waved, then turned to Parker. "Thank you for everything. I hope you have an excellent time this evening. Dinner should be great and the band's not half bad either." Off she went, disappearing into the crowd.

Chloe took his hand. "Okay. What the hell is this?"

His eyes grew impossibly large, but he also had that adorable look of bemusement on his face. Chloe wanted to kiss it away, but she also kind of hoped it would still be there when she was done. "You're going to have to be more specific."

"You invite me to this event, but you don't tell me a thing about your involvement with it. It's kind of a date, but not really a date, but then you tell Jillian that I am, in fact, your date."

He grinned and tugged her closer until they were standing toe-to-toe. "You look good enough to eat in that dress."

She fought a smile, and that was futile, but none of it changed the fact that he was ignoring what she'd said. "That's not much of an explanation."

He turned and started for the darker recesses of the room, bringing Chloe along with him. Once they were in a quiet corner, he reached out and took a tendril of her hair between his fingers, tugging it down and draping it across the pale skin of her cleavage. His knuckles grazed the sensitive area, bringing her to life in a way she hadn't been mere moments ago. "Be my date, Chloe."

She nearly went weak in the knees. "I thought we decided this was a bad idea. You. Me. Our parents."

He shook his head, looking deeply into her eyes. "We didn't decide that. You did. And I'm tired of thinking of our parents. Or anyone else, for that matter. Everyone else can go away as far as I'm concerned."

"For the sake of argument, let's say that we're ignoring everyone else. What does that mean? What do you want?"

He arched both eyebrows at her and dropped his

chin. It made his lower lip pop out in a way that only made Chloe want to bite it. "I think you already know the answer to that question."

"Sex. You want sex."

He shook his head, taking her by surprise. "I want *you*."

She swallowed hard. "You do?"

"Don't you feel like we have unfinished business? We barely got started in Miami."

A white-hot thrill raced through her. She wasn't sure she could take more of Parker, but she wanted to take the risk. She hadn't wanted a man like this in so long. Possibly ever. "Are you asking me to come to your place?"

"Not sure I can wait that long." His eyes scanned the room.

"What are you saying?"

"Let me show you."

"In here?"

"I might be dumb, but I'm not stupid."

Chloe bit down on her lower lip. Were they on the same page? Did he know that she wanted to tear into him the way he apparently wanted to tear into her? "Then where?"

"I know a quiet spot." Taking her hand, he led her through one of the side exits. They spilled out into a hall with a luxurious seating area and soft lighting. He wasted no time, taking her in his arms and spinning her until her back was pressed to the wall.

Chloe's mouth quivered with anticipation of a kiss, but he went for her neck first, caressing her delicate skin with his warm lips. She nearly climaxed from that one kiss, closing her eyes, knocking her head back and exhaling in a soft moan. She flattened her palms in the center of his back, wanting him closer to her.

"This is what I want from you, Chloe. The heat." He trailed his mouth along her collarbone, then began moving lower, to the top of her cleavage. He pressed in closer to her, then lifted his head and looked down the hall. He tugged down the front of her dress on one side until her breast was free from the garment.

The cooler air hit her skin in an exhilarating rush. She immediately stiffened. "Parker. Someone will see."

"It's fine. We're alone." He lowered his head and drew her nipple into his mouth, swirling his tongue around the tight bud.

Any determination Chloe had to argue with him disappeared in smoke. If he kept doing what he was doing to her, she didn't care if the entire ballroom of guests watched them. "Parker. Let's go then. Let's get out of here."

He groaned and took one of her hands, lifting her arm above her head and pinning it against the wall. "I'm having too much fun. You're so hot, Chloe. I can't wait to bury myself inside of you." He punctuated the statement with a forceful kiss, his tongue warm and wet and sinful. There was no mistaking what he was after and Chloe wanted to give it to him all night long. He tightened his grip on her wrist, letting her know that she was at his mercy, then he took his other hand and slipped it through the slit on the side of her dress.

"Parker…" she said between their lips.

"Shh. One more minute," he said slipping his fingers into the front of her panties.

Chloe was fighting that whole weak-knee situation again. Honestly, every muscle in her body was quivering with anticipation while struggling to keep her upright. She closed her eyes and luxuriated in the feel of his finger against her center, as he rubbed in tight, fast circles. The tension was coiling so fast, her breaths cut so short that she didn't know what to do. She couldn't have an orgasm in the hall of a five-star hotel, could she? The courtyard in Miami had been one thing. This was another. There was no time for an answer as she felt the peak rocket through her like white lightning. She kissed Parker harder, if only to stifle the moans fighting their way out of her as her entire body shuddered with pleasure.

He ran his lips along her neck again and discreetly removed one hand from between her legs, and the other let go of her wrist. Chloe tugged up the bodice of her dress to cover herself and avoid walking away from this situation while showing a bit too much skin. Parker angled his body to shield her from anyone who might wander down to where they were.

"I can't believe you did that," she said.

"I couldn't help it."

She placed her hand on his chest, smoothing it over the fine fabric of his jacket. She was caught between too many thoughts, but the one that rang loudest in her head was that she needed to be alone with him. Truly alone. But there were a few things standing in the way. "I think we should stay at the event. Let you bask in the glow of your accomplishments."

"That's sweet of you, but no. I've made my appearance. I've talked to the people I needed to see."

"But Jillian bragged about the dinner. And she said the band was good. Don't you want to dance?" She trailed her finger down his lapel.

"I can think of far better things you and I can do together, Chloe."

"If we're going to leave, I need to find Alex and tell her what's going on."

He drew in a deep breath through his nose, seeming frustrated. "Can't you text her?"

"I'll call her. That's more thoughtful." Chloe dug her phone out of the small evening bag she'd brought, seeing that Alex had already left her a text. Chloe must not have heard the notification while Parker had her in the throes of passion. "She beat me to it. Apparently she's leaving with Ryder. Interesting." *Good for Alex.*

"Let's get out of here. Now." Parker slipped his cell from his pocket and tapped out a message. "My driver should be downstairs in a few minutes."

"How far is your apartment?"

"I think the more pressing question is how private is the back of my limo?"

Nine

Parker was barely holding it together as he and Chloe climbed into the back of his limousine. He had an erection so fierce that he could hardly believe he had any brain function. It had been a real feat to make it through the hotel lobby discreetly. *Thank God for this stupid tux jacket.* It hid a multitude of sins.

"Home, Mr. Sullivan?" Benny asked.

"Yes," Parker answered, glancing over at Chloe. She was sitting right next to him, so beautiful and sexy it boggled the mind.

"Right away," Benny replied. Without needing to be asked, he raised the partition between the two sections of the car.

Chloe didn't wait to move. She slipped her hand

into the hair at the nape of his neck and pulled him closer, kissing him with that mouth he found so disarming. It was her turn to be in charge and she did exactly that, rolling to her hip, then pulling her lips from his and surprising the hell out of him by kneeling on the floor before him. She rolled her hand over his crotch, lightly rubbing the underside of his dick, driving him mad. She peered up at him, her eyes dark in the soft light of the limo, drawing him in like no woman ever had before. "I need to take care of you."

Parker wasn't about to argue as he slid his hips closer to her and leaned back. He loved seeing her fingers unzip his pants, but it was even better when she tugged down the front of his boxer briefs and took him in her hand. He groaned when she took that first stroke, giving him a tiny bit of relief while making him even harder. The pain and the pleasure… what a delicious mix.

He closed his eyes for a moment as she took him in her mouth. So warm and luscious, hot and wet. With every pass, the tension wrapped itself around him a little tighter and he found it more impossible to bear. He dug his fingers into her hair and curled them into her scalp, rubbing with just enough force to tell her how much she was driving him wild, but also how happy she was making him. This was somehow hotter than Miami, which he found nearly impossible to believe. Miami had been ridiculously hot. But this… Well, perhaps it was the familiarity they had now. Or maybe it was simply because he knew now that she couldn't resist him. She had to have him. Just like he had to have her.

He opened his eyes, only to see that she was looking up at him as her lips rode up and down his length. It was so hot it felt criminal, and yet, there was this tenderness to Chloe that always took his breath away. She was soft, even when she tried to show the world a hard exterior. "I want you, Chloe. Right now. In this car." Taking a cursory glance out the window, he knew that they had a good ten minutes before they would get to his building. Plenty of time, especially considering how primed they both were.

She very slowly dragged her lips along his erection, then gently let him go. "Are you sure? In here?"

"I've never been more sure of anything in my life."

Her eyes lit up with mischief. "I've never had sex in a limo."

"First time for everything."

She climbed back up on the seat and hitched her dress up high, revealing her creamy thighs. He flashed back to that moment when he first saw her get out of the car at his dad's house and he'd first realized he wanted her. His hips tightened as he got the first glimpse of her lacy ice blue panties. Sexy and sweet. That was Chloe. She inched them down her legs and placed them on the seat, then gathered her dress in her hands and straddled Parker's lap. He sort of hated that there was so much fabric between them, but he also sort of loved it. Mere minutes ago, she'd been in a ballroom with the wealthiest of New

York City, looking as proper as a woman could look. Only he got to see the side of Chloe that was so hot and dangerous.

He guided himself inside her and she sank down on him, wrapping him up in her velvety warmth. He was immediately plunged into a world where only she existed, where he felt like he was going to rocket into space from mere seconds inside her. The pressure that had built up in him already was like a bottle of expensive champagne that had been shaken within an inch of its life. He was teetering on the brink already. So close. Too damn close.

Chloe lowered her head and kissed him as she rocked her hips back and forth. Her breaths were short and choppy and he sensed the restlessness in her. He felt it as he wrapped his arms around her waist and pulled her closer. As fun and hot and dangerous as this was, he couldn't wait to get her in his apartment and fully undressed, get the full view of her beautiful naked body as he drove her to her peak again and again. It was the start of the weekend, he reminded himself. They could wear each other out until neither had a thing to give. Then they could sleep and start again.

Chloe buried her face in his neck and began rocking harder. "I'm so close," she moaned against his skin.

"Come for me, Chloe. Come so hard. I want to see it on your face and hear it in your voice and most important, I want to feel it."

It was either something he said or something he

did that made her body freeze after only one more thrust. She knocked back her head, and he felt her gather hard around him, just as he'd begged her to do. That was all it took to propel him over the edge, desperate for breath and yet somehow not caring about things like oxygen. It felt so good. Too good.

Chloe rolled her head to the side, then back forward, collapsing against him. "You are unbelievable."

Did she really feel that way about him? Because he'd been feeling that way about her. He'd been so sure he had her all figured out from the beginning— the uptight society girl who only did things that were safe. But Chloe had a real adventurous streak, even if she didn't know it. He found it absolutely thrilling, wondering what they could do together next. He clasped both sides of her face with his hands and kissed her softly. "Just wait until I get you inside." He glanced out the car window. "We'll be at my building in a few minutes."

"I'd better get presentable." She climbed off his lap and began to straighten her dress.

Parker got his own clothes situated, then reached for Chloe's panties at the same moment she did. "You don't need these," he said.

"Of course I do. Plus, they were super expensive."

He tucked them into the pocket of his tux jacket. "I'll just hold on to them."

"Why?"

"Because it's going to be way too fun riding the elevator of my incredibly fancy apartment building, just knowing that you aren't wearing any panties. If I'm lucky, we'll run into one of my neighbors."

She leaned closer and kissed him. "You're bad."

"Only if you want me to be."

Benny dropped them off in the parking garage, and Parker wasted no time getting them to the elevator and up to his apartment. One of the things that had sold him on this unit was that right inside the door was the payoff—you walked right into his sprawling living room, which had the same breathtaking view of the Hudson River as his home gym and bedroom.

"Wow, Parker. Just wow." The midnight blue sky, the dark ripples of the river and the twinkle of city lights clearly called to Chloe as she seemed to float ahead, drawn to the windows.

"You like it?" He took off his jacket and tossed it onto one of the couches, unbuttoning his shirt cuffs, then down the front. He wanted Chloe to take off his clothes, but he also didn't want to wait to have her glorious naked body pressed hard against his.

"I love it. It's a million-dollar view."

"It's 2.4, but who's counting?" He mumbled and he stood right behind her and placed his hands on her hips, kissing the back of her neck as he drew the zipper of her dress down to her waist. Every brush of his skin against hers was so heavenly, it made him hard as a rock from the word *go*.

She turned in his arms, clutching her dress to her chest. "Oh. Your shirt is off." At first she sounded surprised, but the look in her eyes spoke of her appreciation. Her touch as she rolled her fingertips over his shoulders told him everything else he needed to know. She wanted him just as badly as he wanted her. As she slowly unfurled her arms and let her dress slump to the floor, he drank in her exquisite curves. Every swell so luscious and begging for his touch. She smiled. "Now we're even?"

"Almost." He loved seeing her in his apartment, flawless and naked and vulnerable in front of a huge window. She'd let down her guard again and it was such a damn turn-on to know that she trusted him That she cared more about being with him than about being appropriate or doing what others expected of her. He shucked his pants and finally, he had everything he wanted right before him.

"Your bedroom?"

He shook his head. "In a little bit. Right now I want you here. Right here." He lifted her up, his fingers sinking in the luxurious flesh of her butt as he thumped her back against the wall next to the window. He positioned himself at her entrance and drove inside, sending a message, strong and forceful. Chloe wrapped her legs around his waist and he marveled at how perfectly they fit together, how completely she wrapped him up in her unspeakable warmth. Her hands clasped his neck, urging his mouth down to hers. The kiss was hot and wet, just like Chloe. Parker felt like the luckiest damn guy in the entire world.

He slid one hand to the small of her back, pressing hard to make her arch into him. He dropped his head, taking one of her pert nipples between his lips, sucking hard and looping his tongue. He felt her body tighten as he tasted her, a rich reward for every bit of pleasure he was giving her. The blissful pleasure was building in him fast, and as good as this was, he knew he could do better. He knew he could go deeper.

He pulled her close and lifted her body from against the wall, turning and taking a step, then setting her down on a desk that was more for looks than actual work. He loosened his grip on her and she eased back, propping herself up with her arms. It gave him the most mind-blowing view—Chloe's breasts gently bobbing as he drove into her again and again. He made every stroke count, long and hard and slow. The pleasure was so immense it was difficult to wrap his mind around it. So he didn't try to think. He instead studied the beautiful look on her face as her eyes drifted shut and she dropped her head to one side and soft moans left her luscious lips.

"Are you close, Chloe?" he asked, amazed by just how rough his voice sounded.

She nodded, eyes closed. "So close. Ridiculously close."

He knew exactly how to get her where she needed to go, and he slipped his thumb against her apex and began rotating in small circles, using delicate pressure. She gasped the instant he touched her there. Her eyes flew open.

"Oh. Wow."

He felt her tighten around him. Then again. "Yeah."

"So good. It feels so… Good."

He smiled, sensing how close she was to unraveling, and he studied with great satisfaction that moment when she finally gave way. She tossed her head back and called out, digging her heels into the back of his thighs, right below his ass. He lowered his torso and pressed his chest against her breasts, kissing her deeply as the waves of pleasure shot through him. He unleashed himself into her in fierce and unrelenting pulses. It was as hot as anything he could have imagined. He collapsed forward, burrowing his head in her neck as she bucked against his hips a few times. Parker had a pretty big sexual appetite, but he was going to need at least a half hour before he could go again.

Chloe's stomach rumbled and she giggled into his chest. "Sorry about that."

"Are you hungry?"

"Starving."

He smiled and pressed a soft kiss to her lips. "I can take care of that."

"I have no doubt. You seem to be able to take care of just about everything."

Chloe was slowly drifting into consciousness, but she didn't open her eyes. Not yet. She needed a moment to wrap her mind around the way she was feeling right now. There was no mental guessing game like there had been in Miami—she knew she was in Parker's bed. She might not have his skin against hers or feel him shifting in the bed, but she sensed his presence. She breathed in his incredible smell. And of course, there were the aftershocks of last night, still reverberating in her body. He was a force of nature, and she'd been right there in the eye of that very sexy storm.

As she pried her eyes open, she realized she was alone, so she took a moment to soak up her first view of his bedroom in daylight. It had been too dark and she'd been too wrapped up in Parker the first time she'd walked into his inner sanctum. Straight ahead from the foot of the bed was an entire wall of windows, offering spectacular views of the Hudson River. It was hard to look away from the view, but she did take her chance to peruse his decor choices. In one corner was a comfortable armchair of cognac-brown leather with nail-head trim, dressed with a gray wool throw and a dark wooden side table. Chloe could imagine curling up there with a good book on a rainy day. The walls were blanketed in pale gray, the bed dressed in crisp white and the floors ebony-stained wood. The feel of the space was nothing short of pure luxury and sophistication. Chloe was impressed, which was saying a lot, because she'd been in plenty of beautiful rooms in her life. But between the revelations at the fundraiser and everything that happened the minute they walked out of that ballroom, Parker continued to leave her in awe.

Just then, he appeared in the doorway. "You're up."

A smile bloomed on her face, pulling her cheeks high and her lips wide. "I am."

He walked around to her side of the bed, looking

like everything a woman could want, in black-and-gray-plaid pajama pants without a shirt, holding a cup of coffee for her. "I brought the liquid of life."

She scooted up in bed and wrapped her hands around the mug, taking a long sip before setting it aside. "Thank you so much."

He settled his sights directly on her. "How are you doing?"

"I feel great." In all honesty, she felt better than that. She was relaxed, which was not her normal state.

"You sure?"

"I don't understand the question."

He pulled a knee up onto the bed and peered even more seriously into her eyes. "You aren't freaking out. I sort of expected you to panic this morning. Jump out of bed and start gathering your clothes in a hurry, telling me you had a lot you had to do today."

Her normal reaction to most things Parker accused her of was to deny, deny, deny. But he wasn't wrong about this. She felt no need to race out the door. Waking up in Parker's bed in New York was *not* like it had been in Miami. What had made the difference? It was only a week later, and the other obstacles between them had not changed. *Last night made the difference.* "I'm just going to be totally honest about this, okay?"

"Please."

"Being with you at the fundraiser last night made me see you in a very different light."

"Plenty of people with money are involved with charities."

"It's more than that, though. You don't just contribute or raise money. You give with time and effort. Writing a big check takes very little effort. It's not so easy to show up in a real way. A way that requires commitment."

He granted her a fragment of a grin, but he also let out a doubtful laugh. "I think you're giving me too much credit."

"I'm not. Believe me. In my line of work, I see lots of people do performative charity work. Show up for a photo op or make a big deal about a donation. You don't do any of those things. If anything, you're entirely too humble about it."

"You're reading too much into it."

"I don't think I am. You know, everyone in this city loves to paint you as just another wealthy, arrogant, hopelessly handsome guy. But I'm starting to think that's all an act."

"The handsome part is not an act. I come by that naturally." He bounced both eyebrows at her.

Chloe laughed and the next thing she knew, Parker tackled her, pushing her back on the mattress, then rolling to his back so she was lying on top of him.

"I want you," he said.

"I have coffee breath."

"Don't care." He kissed her softly, digging his fingers into her hair.

She thought she might pass out, even though she was in a prone position. "Last night was amazing."

"It was."

"I can't believe what we did in the hall." She dropped her head, still feeling a bit embarrassed.

"You're not much for public displays of affection?" He threaded his fingers through her hair.

"That was not PDA. I'm pretty sure that was a misdemeanor."

"It was fun, though. Super fun." He kissed her again. "I love watching you come."

She hated that it was her immediate response, but she blushed. She'd never been with a guy who was such an open book when it came to sex, a man who was so at ease with talking about it. Chloe had never been a talker, especially when it came to intimacy. She'd always been wound too tight, too afraid she was going to do the wrong thing or get hurt. Parker was pulling at her strings, slowly loosening the ties that bound her up and kept her life manageable. Under any other circumstances, this might be a terrifying thought. But his laid-back, capable manner took the edge off that fear. If she added in the temptation of being with him, he was pretty damn impossible to resist.

Just then, an unfamiliar sound came from somewhere in the room. A yap. A bark? "What was that?" she asked.

Parker smiled. "Blue, are you jealous?" he asked.

Now Chloe was even more confused. "Blue?"

"That's my dog. Hold on." He shifted out from under Chloe and scooted to the edge of the bed, where he leaned over and reached down to the floor.

He rolled back over and plopped an adorable dark gray bulldog in front of Chloe. "Meet Blue."

The dog sat, looking back and forth between Parker and her, quirking its ears and seeming unsure of what to do.

"It's okay." He scratched the dog behind its ears. "Chloe won't bite."

Blue carefully approached Chloe while Parker settled back in, lying on his side and propping his head up with his hand.

Chloe reached out to pet Blue. "He's adorable. You didn't tell me you had a dog."

"Blue's a she, actually. And she's a Frenchie. Very low maintenance. She's basically a dog-shaped cat. Rarely barks. Very affectionate. She was asleep in her crate when we got back last night. I have someone check in on her twice a day. Sometimes I bring her to the office."

"She sounds like the perfect pet. She also sounds like a lot of work."

"She's worth it. It gets lonely living by yourself."

Yet another moment for Parker to take her by surprise. "I guess I thought you liked being on your own."

"I'd say that I'm more used to being alone, not that I actually like it."

"Because of your perpetual bachelorhood?" Chloe asked as Blue butted her hand for more head rubs.

"It's always been that way for me. The whole time I was growing up. I was an only child, my dad traveled a ton for work and my mom was always sick."

Chloe had wondered about his mother. He never spoke of her. "The whole time you were growing up?"

"She passed away when I was fourteen. She was diagnosed with cancer when I was little, but she fought like hell for ten years."

Her heart went out to Parker so much that she felt an actual ache in the center of her chest. "I'm so sorry. My dad died when I was really young, and it was very sudden, so I don't really remember him. That must have been so hard to watch your mom struggle with her illness. Is that why you're so involved with the hospital?"

He nodded slowly, looking resigned. "It is. I think I was just old enough when she died that I knew I had to do something about it. And once I got involved, I couldn't help but want to stay in it."

"Like I said before, your generosity amazes me."

"I get something out of it, too. It's extremely rewarding."

Chloe needed something like that in her life, too. Her time was consumed by work, her friends and her mom. But she probably spent a little too much time on the first one, and not nearly enough on the last two. Taylor and Alex were always complaining that they didn't get to see her very often, and come to think of it, her mom often said the same thing. "You mentioned that your dad usually accompanies you to that event. Why not this year?"

"He said something about them only wanting a

check from him. I don't think that's true, but it's what he seems to think."

"How's he handling the divorce?"

"Fine, I guess. I told him I hired you for the Marcus job, by the way."

This was a revelation Chloe had not expected. She might have worried that this meant the news would get back to her mom, but she knew that her mom would likely never speak to George again. "What did he say?"

"He was thankful. He's hoping it might make your mom hate him a little less. I don't think he's happy with the way things ended. It didn't sound good."

"If it helps at all, my mom already has a new guy. Sounds like she's moving on from your dad, which I guess is good."

"Funny that you should mention that. My dad and I talked about the idea of him moving on, too. As in I suggested he not move on and instead spend some time being on his own."

"Do you think he'll take your advice?"

"Hard to know. He plays all of that very close to the vest. Maybe that's why it bothers me so much when he decides to get married again. I never see it coming. And then it's *boom*. Wedding bells."

"I always see it coming. It's like watching a very slow car crash."

"Why do you think she's so ready to fall in love?"

"I don't know. The whole idea of rushing to get your heart broken seems so foolish to me." The minute she answered the question, the things Alexandra had said to her the night before began to rifle through her head.

"I'm not going to break your heart, Chloe. Just so you know."

She drew in a deep breath, thinking about Parker in the context of everything she believed about love and commitment. She really liked spending time with him, but it was hard to envision it ever lasting more than a few days. Either she'd go back to panicking or he'd get distracted by another woman or perhaps they'd both get so wrapped up in their jobs that they'd forget what it was that they saw in each other. So maybe it was a good approach to simply enjoy her time with him and not be so serious about everything. Have some fun. Then leave when it was time to go. "Good. Although I wasn't going to let you, either."

Blue got up from her spot next to Chloe, wandered to the end of the bed, jumped on to an upholstered bench at the foot of the mattress, then hopped down to the floor. That left nothing between Parker and Chloe but his pajama pants, the thin silky sheet covering her. They had the rest of the morning and an entire afternoon if they wanted to take it.

"I have no doubt that you'll put up your armor when you need to."

She slid a finger beneath the edge of the bedsheet and pulled it away, revealing her naked body to him. It was the sort of bold move she didn't make, but it felt so natural with Parker. It was the only thing that made sense. "I'm not wearing any armor right now."

"I see that." His hand rolled over her bare hip, then he slipped it between her legs. In a split second, she was at his mercy.

"Parker—" she gasped, amazed by how quickly he had her close to the edge.

His face drifted to hers, kissing her hard. "Yes?"

"Please don't stop."

"Whatever you want. For as long as you want it."

She rolled to her back with only one thought on her mind—*he* was everything she wanted. For now.

Ten

A weekend with Parker turned into a week. Which turned into another week. And another after that. When Chloe wasn't overanalyzing, it was *perfect*. Absolute bliss. Her pulse picked up every time she saw him, but he also had a calming effect on her. He got her to unwind, mostly because there wasn't another option with Parker. As intense and focused as he could be, he was simply a very laid-back guy. He didn't let things eat at him the way Chloe did. His work was a bear just like hers was, but at night when they were together he didn't let the worries from that day consume him. A glass of wine, some TV and snuggle time with Blue, and it was like there was no stress in his life at all. He would give her that look, the one that said he wanted her, and the next thing she knew the entire world fell away. How did he do that? Chloe wasn't entirely sure. All she could do was adopt his approach to life and hope that at some point, she could stop being so worried about everything.

Of course, it wasn't as simple as that. Spending every spare minute with Parker meant that her mom and her friends were feeling ignored, and that piled on the stress for Chloe. Taylor and Alex wanted updates. They wanted to know the state of things between Parker and her, and Chloe simply didn't know how to answer that question, other than to say that they were happy. As for her mom, Chloe found herself immensely thankful her mom had a new guy. Whoever he was, he was occupying a good deal of her time. But that didn't keep her mother from noticing when Chloe hadn't come to visit.

"Another weekend gone without seeing your face," her mom said over speakerphone as Chloe was getting settled in her office on a Monday morning. "I'm worried I'll forget what you look like."

"Mom, come on. Please don't give me a guilt trip. You know I'm busy. It's just the way things are."

Forrest appeared in the doorway to Chloe's office with an armful of files and she waved him in.

"It's my right to point out that your priorities aren't in order," her mother said.

"I run my own PR company. I assure you that I am only making time for things that are immensely important."

"I find it very difficult to believe you're working nonstop every weekend. There's something else going on. There's a man, isn't there? And you're keeping him from me."

Chloe and Forrest made eye contact, and a distinct mix of shock and horror came over his face. "I'll come back later," he whispered.

Sorry, she mouthed.

Chloe took her mom off speaker and held the phone to her ear. "Do we really have to have this conversation right now? It's nine-thirty on a Monday morning, I have a million emails to answer, and client meetings after that."

"Just answer the question. Yes or no. Is there a man who's occupying your time?"

"And what if there is?"

"Then I want to meet him. That's all. I want to know his name and who he is and what he does."

Oh, no. That is not happening. "I don't know *your* boyfriend's name. I'm not the only one who's hiding things."

"So this mystery man *is* your boyfriend?"

Dammit. Chloe could hardly believe she'd not only walked into that, she'd created the problem for herself. Another tide of guilt washed over her. She'd known this reckoning might come someday, but she'd also argued with herself that it was okay to put it off. She kept waiting for something to go wrong with Parker, so she could save herself the headache, and most important, shield her mom from the sense of betrayal she would inevitably express. The trouble was the perfection of being with Parker. Nothing had gone wrong. He managed to do everything right. "Yes. There's a guy. But I'm not ready for you to meet him."

"Is it the fling you mentioned at brunch after your trip to Miami?"

She was already precariously close to lying to her mom. She had to be forthcoming about some things. "Yes."

"You've been back for over a month. That's not a fling."

"Then we'll pick another term for it." Chloe struggled for the right word. Affair? Tryst? Liaison? None of those felt right. They were all so minimizing. What she had with Parker was more.

"It sounds to me like a relationship. Which brings me back to my original point. I'd like to know who he is. I'd like to know about it if you're falling in love."

Chloe felt as though her heart had frozen in the center of her chest. Speaking of uncomfortable words—that one went at the top of the list. "I promise to tell you if I fall in love." *That's a long time down the road. If at all.*

"I should certainly hope so."

"I really have to go, Mom. Maybe we can have breakfast one day this week? My afternoons are full of meetings."

"It will have to be today or tomorrow. I'm going out of town for a few days with Gavin."

"Gavin? The new boyfriend?"

"Yes. Gavin Goldstein. He's in art and antiquities."

"I know who he is. I've been to his gallery. I've

also seen his family's wing at the Met." It was amazing the way her mom attracted rich and powerful men like flies.

"How about tomorrow? Nine o'clock at Muffy's? We'll put it on the books so you can't bow out of it?"

"Sure. I can do that." Chloe wanted to see her mom, but she definitely dreaded the fifth degree she would undoubtedly get. At least she could put it off for twenty-four hours.

"Wonderful. I'll see you then."

Chloe hung up the phone and Forrest reappeared mere seconds later. "I'm sorry I was in the room when your mom decided to put you on the spot."

"I actually think it's good for me when you hear some of her craziness. It helps me to know that it really happened and I didn't just imagine it."

Forrest laughed quietly. "Oh, it definitely happened."

"Is there something you need?"

"Yes. Fran Lipman over at *American Entertainment* magazine sent you an email about a piece she's running, but she also called to follow up. I think she's eager to get an answer. It sounds like she had someone bow out. I promised her I'd bring it to your attention right away."

Chloe immediately went to her laptop. Fran was an old friend and would often send opportunities Chloe's way. "Okay. Two secs." It only took a minute for her to find the email and read through it. "She's doing a series on celebrities who live in famous American cities. And you're right. She had someone bow out, so she's desperate. The only hitch is she wants someone who isn't too horribly controversial."

"That rules out Dakota," Forrest said. Indeed, she was back to shoplifting again.

Chloe mentally ran down her current client list, but she felt as though she already had the perfect person for it. "The natural answer is Marcus Grant. Miami is on the list of available cities. And his controversy was a blip on the map."

"We aren't representing him anymore though, right? That project is complete."

"No, we aren't. But I'm sure Parker would love it."

Forrest nodded slowly. "Right. His agent. Parker Sullivan."

She couldn't ignore the leading tone in her voice. "Forrest, say whatever it is that you want to say."

Now he was shaking his head. "I would never comment on your personal life."

"What if I asked you to?"

"I'm not taking that bait. All I'll say is that I like him a lot more than I thought I would."

You and me both. "Good to know." She returned her sights to her computer. "Can you think of anyone else we can bring to Fran?"

"No. I can't."

"Okay, then. I'll get back to them as soon as I run it past Parker."

"If they call again, I'll let them know as much." Forrest disappeared through the door.

Chloe called Parker right away.

"Hey there, beautiful," he said when he picked up. "Is everything okay?"

She smiled. Having that sort of attention from him was like standing in the sun on a beautiful summer day. "Everything's fine. I wanted to run something by you."

"Please."

She gave him the rundown on the magazine piece. "I was thinking that Marcus and Miami would be perfect for it. A good-looking all-American athlete, living in a stunning house in a great city, with a promising career ahead of him. And it'll hit newsstands right around the start of his rookie season, so it could be perfect."

"It sounds amazing. What would we need to do?"

"As near as I can tell, it's a quick photo shoot and a short Q and A. Nothing too taxing."

"That's fantastic. Which of your clients are you submitting?"

"None, actually. They only wanted one name, and I think Marcus is perfect for this."

"Don't you have a client that could use a little positive publicity? You just spent the second half of last week dealing with Dakota Ladd's return to shoplifting."

"I don't think Dakota is ready for this. It's baby steps for her right now. Do you not think Marcus will want to do it?"

"No. I do. And if he doesn't want to, I'll make him do it. I'm just surprised since Marcus isn't your client anymore. I haven't paid you anything beyond your fee for the Miami interviews."

Confusion began to cloud Chloe's thoughts, and she really wished she had a better understanding of her place in Parker's life, the way she fit—or didn't—into his life. "I don't need you to pay me. I wanted to do it."

"Oh, okay. I don't want to take advantage of you being…" He hesitated.

What? Me being what?

"I mean, I don't want to take advantage of our relationship."

At least that word gave her a tiny bit of clarity. "I want to help you and Marcus. But I also don't want to overstep."

"It's not possible for you to overstep. It was very, very sweet and kind of you to do this. Thank you."

Chloe felt as though she'd just gone for a ride on a roller coaster. One minute she was happy, the next she felt like the bottom had dropped out of her stomach. Yes, she'd been returned to the start, where she felt safe, but she wasn't sure how many more times she could take that. "You're welcome. I'll email you the details."

"Perfect. I'll see you tonight?"

The words that should have been tacked on at the end of his question were *at home*, but his apartment was not home for Chloe, even though it felt that way. "Yes. I should be there by seven. What do you want to do for dinner?"

"Takeout? Maybe Italian?"

"The last time we ordered Italian, we were eating cold pasta carbonara at midnight because we were otherwise occupied." She grinned so wide she had to bury her head in her hand. That had been a wicked hot night. Right after their dinner had been delivered, Parker cast her a look in the kitchen that made food a total afterthought. Before she knew what was happening, they were kissing, clothes were strewn all over the floor and he had Chloe calling out his name from her perch on the kitchen counter.

"If we get a replay of that night, I definitely want Italian."

She laughed. She might be questioning many things right now, but she never doubted her desire to be with him. "I can't wait."

"I can't wait either."

Chloe hung up and turned in her chair and stared out her office window, trying to process her conversations from the last hour. She was in deep with Parker. So deep, even when she'd told herself hundreds of times that she'd never get there. That she wouldn't allow herself to go there. Was it genetic? Had she caught what her mother so often fell prey to? It was possible. They were alike in many ways. Could she be in love with Parker? She closed her eyes and drew in a deep breath. *Just get back to work. You can worry about everything with Parker and your mom later.*

Parker had to take a minute after he got off the phone with Chloe. Coming close to saying *girlfriend* was one thing. Nearly referring to his apartment as home was another. But what really confused him was the three little words that popped into his head right before he hung up. *I love you*. Where in the hell had that come from?

A knock came at his office door, which was open. "Mr. Sullivan?" Luna, the office manager, popped her head inside, carrying a large three-ring binder. "Sorry to interrupt."

Parker shook his head to clear his thoughts. "No. No. It's fine. What is it?"

"You asked for these college basketball scouting reports?"

Parker needed to get back on his game, and back to work. "Right. Thank you." He took the file from Luna, but as she walked away, he realized he could get some other information from her. "Luna, can I ask you a question?"

She turned back to him. "Sure thing. What's up?"

"If a guy was going to buy a woman a piece of jewelry that said I like you a lot but not necessarily more than that, where would he go?"

Luna arched both eyebrows at him. "You do realize that not every woman thinks of a gift of jewelry as a promise, right? If it's not a diamond ring, I think you're safe."

He felt like an idiot, but that was becoming a familiar feeling when it came to these matters. "So I can just go to Tiffany? Somewhere like that?"

She nodded. "I'm sure they'll hook you up with the perfect thing."

"Great. Thank you."

Parker spent his entire workday with electricity coursing through his veins. This was what Chloe did to him. She lit the match. She started the fire. She made him feel alive. And that was just from a phone call, which was a remarkable thing.

He was still amazed she'd passed along the publicity opportunity for Marcus. The Chloe of a month ago would not have done that. Or if she had, she would have made Parker squirm for it, at least a little bit. He couldn't deny that she'd taken a surprising role in his life—she made him feel good about everything. Most important, he couldn't imagine his day-to-day without her. Looking back on the way he'd been before Chloe? It all seemed so empty. He'd been so busy charging through life, working hard and playing harder, a long string of women who meant very little to him, all because he'd been so dedicated to the idea of not making the same mistakes his father had. Chloe was the one person who'd gotten to him. Her softer side made him appreciate the little things, like having someone other than his dog to be with at the end of a long day.

He left the office early and Benny drove him to the flagship Tiffany store on 57th Street, where he popped in to buy his gift for Chloe. The store was much busier than he'd expected, quite packed with shoppers. But there was one salesperson who had just completed a sale—a gray-haired man in glasses and wearing an impeccable suit with a name tag that simply said *Mr. Russell*.

"May I help you, sir?" he asked. His British accent surprised Parker, but it only added to the distinguished air about the man.

"I need a gift. For my girlfriend." Finally, Parker had just come out with it. The relief registered in his body immediately. He and Chloe had been wading through murky waters, and she really struggled with all of that, especially the potential fallout from her mom. But it was time to be definitive about their relationship, especially when he knew it was true. She had become his girlfriend.

"I see. Special occasion?"

It was early April and Chloe's birthday wasn't until summer. With no romantic holiday in sight, Parker had to admit his true aim. "No. I just need her to know that she's really important to me."

Mr. Russell grinned, which Parker had to admire. He'd probably heard hundreds of men say something along those lines, and the sentiment apparently hadn't lost its luster. "Do you know what you're looking for?"

Not knowing exactly what he was looking for, Parker was left to explain to the salesman what Chloe meant to him. "I don't know, exactly. We've only been together a little more than a month." *But it feels like I've known her forever.* "She's so beautiful, with flowing red hair and rosy cheeks." *She's perfect.* "And when she laughs, it's like the whole world stops." *At least it does for me.*

"And her name?"

"Chloe."

"Chloe sounds like a very special woman," the salesman said. "And how much were you looking to spend?"

"Oh. If it were up to me, I'd spend a lot. But I don't think she would want anything too extravagant." *I don't want her to freak out.*

"I have several ideas. Let's see if anything can live up to your lovely lady's beauty." Mr. Russell showed him various bracelets, and earrings, but it was a necklace with a delicate chain and a round pendant studded with diamonds that really caught Parker's eye.

"That one." He tapped the display glass.

"Excellent choice. Might I suggest the rose gold? It can be quite striking on a woman with red hair." Mr. Russell pulled it from the case and presented it on its pale gray velvet stand. It caught the light from every angle, sparkling like crazy.

"Yes. That's it. That's the one." In his mind, he could see Chloe wearing it. He could see her loving it.

"I appreciate your decisiveness. Not every man is so determined with his selection."

Parker took some pride from that. He'd spent his life being noncommittal when it came to expressions of affection. But this felt right. "Thank you."

"Very well then. I'll ring it up and send you on your way." Mr. Russell carefully packed up the necklace.

Parker watched Mr. Russell work, realizing that he reminded him quite a bit of his father, but it was more than the silvery hair. It was the romantic streak. And funnily enough, that was what drew Parker to Mr. Russell. It was what made him like him. Parker might have been too hard on his dad. There was nothing wrong with being soft-hearted when it came to romance. If anything, it was admirable.

Mr. Russell handed over the shopping bag. "I'd love to help you when you bring her in to pick out something for her left ring finger."

Parker laughed quietly. The man's romantic tendencies were no joke. "We'll see how this necklace goes over first."

In the car on the way home, Parker couldn't sit still. Despite the outcome, his conversation with Chloe had been a bit off that morning, the two of them yet again feeling around in the dark, trying to figure out where they stood with each other. Chloe had seemed unsettled and unsure of herself. He'd thought that was just Chloe's normal tendency to overthink everything, but now he was wondering if the thing she was unsure about was him. He took a deep breath and looked out the window as the city whizzed by. He couldn't bring himself to worry about his fate. The one good thing about an expensive piece of jewelry—he'd definitely know how she felt after he gave it to her.

Back at his building and in the elevator on the way up to his floor, Parker's phone beeped with a text. He fished it out of his pocket just as he stepped into his apartment. What he saw on his screen made him freeze right in his tracks. He flashed back to that morning in Miami, when Chloe got a text of a photo she was not eager for the world to see. Because here he was, presented with yet another compromising picture. This one was of Chloe and Parker in the hall outside the fundraiser, her breast peeking out from the confines of her bodice and Parker's hand between her legs.

"How in the hell did anyone take this picture?" he mumbled to himself. He looked at it again. His face was buried in her neck. Her mouth was wide open, her eyes shut tight. *So hot.* And yet, Chloe was going to *freak* when she saw it.

"Parker?" she called. "I just opened a bottle of wine."

Who is this? he quickly typed, then set his laptop bag on the table in the foyer.

It was you all along, wasn't it?

That was all Parker needed to know. It was Little Black Book. It had to be. And they'd finally figured out that it wasn't Chloe who was trying to unmask them, it was him.

"Everything okay?" Chloe asked, poking her head out from the kitchen, holding a glass of wine, with bright eyes and a warm smile on her face. She looked like everything he hadn't known he'd wanted.

He wasn't about to throw that away. He wasn't about to ruin their night, even when the message on his phone screamed for his attention. He suspected Little Black Book might be more bluster than bite.

They'd tried to threaten Chloe with the photo in Miami, and nothing ever came of it. So maybe it was okay if he set this aside until tomorrow. And maybe it was better to ignore it altogether. Was he feeding the beast by engaging? His very hopeful heart said yes.

"Yeah. Yeah. Everything's fine. Just a work thing." He powered down his phone and left it on the table next to his laptop bag, then toted the Tiffany shopping bag to the kitchen. Holding it behind him, he first took his chance to get a kiss from her. "Hi. You look and smell amazing." It was the truth, and he couldn't help but let his lips travel along her jaw, then down one side of her neck. He was such a sucker for her and he knew it.

"Hi yourself." She pecked him on the forehead then poured him a glass of wine. "What are you hiding behind your back?"

He proudly presented the iconic blue bag. "I bought you a gift."

"Tiffany? You didn't. What's this for?" She was grinning from ear to ear as she eagerly took it from him.

"Open it."

She reached inside and pulled out the square flat box, again in the signature Tiffany blue, tied with a white satin ribbon. As she tugged on the tie, her gaze connected with his, making him feel as though he'd made the right decision by giving her this gift. When she lifted the lid, her eyes nearly doubled in size. She took the necklace in her hand, admiring it in the light. "Oh, my God. It's beautiful. Absolutely stunning. I love the rose gold."

He took it from her and stepped behind her to put it on, noticing how his fingers were fumbling with the clasp. His heart, now twice its normal size, was hammering in his chest. It wasn't because he'd worried about whether she'd like it. It was more nervousness over what it all meant to him. He wasn't merely falling for her, he was flat-out head over heels. He knew it with everything in him. "The salesman said it would look pretty with your hair. Now I know he was right." He stood back and took a sip of his wine, admiring her as her fingers ran over the pendant.

"I worry it's too much," she said.

"That's not possible."

"Is it because I did you the favor with Marcus today? Because I told you that I don't expect anything in return. I only did it because I wanted to help."

And I love you for it. The words were right there on his lips, ringing in his head, and running circles in his mind. *I could buy you fifty necklaces and it wouldn't be enough.* Parker wondered how many more realizations he could handle in one night. The voice inside his head kept telling him to level up with Chloe. Yes, the necklace had been a lovely gesture, but what he really needed to do was tell her about the emotion behind the gift. "It's not because of Marcus. It's because of you. And the way you make me feel. It's because of the last month. It's been so incredible."

Chloe tilted her head to one side, narrowing her

sights on him. "It's not like you to make grand statements, Parker. Everything is always so casual with you. Are you feeling okay? Did something happen?"

He reached for her hand. "I nearly called you my girlfriend when we were talking this morning. And I feel like an idiot for not just coming out with it, because the truth is that I think of you that way." He sucked in a deep breath for courage. "This is going to sound crazy. And implausible. But I'm falling for you, Chloe. If I think about tomorrow, I want you there. And the day after that. And the day after that."

For a moment, she stood frozen. The only movement was when she blinked. "I... I don't know what to say."

He sighed and pulled her closer. "It's not what either of us planned. And I don't want you to feel like you owe me anything, but I would like to know how you feel. It doesn't have to be now. But I'd like to know at some point."

She pulled her head back and looked up into his eyes, scanning his face like she was looking for answers. "My mom wants to know who you are."

"What?"

"We talked today. She knows I'm involved with someone. She knows that there's a man who's taking up my time and she said she wants to know who he is. She wants to meet him."

"Right." There was the problem that had been before them all along. Their parents had given them two legacies, neither of which Parker nor Chloe could control. They'd set out a long string of bad examples when it came to love. And then to underscore how ill-equipped they were for commitment, they'd gone and gotten married, only to dissolve it less than a year later. Parker felt fairly sure that he could sway his dad to his side, make him see that what happened with Chloe was completely unplanned. But as for Chloe and her mom, Parker wasn't sure. Chloe had always seemed certain her mother would draw a hard line in the sand. "And do you still feel the same way you felt before? That she'd never be able to get past it?"

A grimace crossed her face and worry made her forehead wrinkle. He hated it when she got stressed like this. He wanted to make it all go away. "Most likely, yes. But I won't know for sure until I say something. Right? I'm having breakfast with her to-morrow."

"You'll tell her then?"

"I guess it's time to just go for it and tell her that you're the guy I'm spending so much time with."

His heart felt as though it might leap out of his chest. "You'd do that for me?"

She nodded. "I don't want to blow up what we have without at least trying to get through to her. She has a new boyfriend, so maybe there's a chance she'll be okay with it."

"One can only hope."

"And I know she wants me to be happy."

"Do I make you happy, Chloe?"

Miraculously, her worried face from a few min-utes ago disappeared, replaced by the glorious expression she wore when she was feeling upbeat and unburdened. "You do. You make me really happy."

From down by his feet, Blue barked. He leaned down and scooped her up. "Chloe and I are trying to have a serious conversation, and you're interrupting," he said to the dog.

Chloe scratched behind Blue's ears. "Maybe she just feels left out. She's always wanting some affection."

"Later." Parker gave Blue a gentle squeeze, then put her down on the floor and reined Chloe in with his arms. "You are the object of my affection, Chloe Burnett. And I hope you let me show you."

"I hope you'll let me do the same. You deserve some sort of thanks for my necklace." She kissed him softly, then drew her finger down the front of his shirt and popped open a button. And another.

They'd had plenty of wild interludes—Miami. The hotel hall. The limo. The living room. But something told him that tonight was for a different locale. He took her hand and began leading her in that direction. "Come on. This way."

"The bedroom?"

"Yes, darling. Tonight is for making love."

Eleven

Chloe woke to the smell of coffee and some very big news waiting for her on her phone.

She had a text from Forrest. Liam's wife had her baby. A little girl.

She sat up in bed and smiled. That's wonderful. Can you send a gift basket?

Already ordered. FYI, car service doesn't have another driver today. Big conference at Marriott.

It's okay. Going to breakfast with my mom. I'll cab it to the office. In before noon.

See you soon.

She pulled back the covers, ducked into Parker's bathroom to pee, then headed for the kitchen. On her way, she heard Parker's voice.

"Blue? What did you do?" His tone was near panicked.

Chloe hurried up. "Everything okay?"

Parker was crouched over the dog. On the floor were tiny bits of Tiffany blue. "She ate the bag, the box your necklace came in and the ribbon."

Blue looked at Parker, then looked at Chloe. She seemed fine. "Do you think she'll be okay?"

"Maybe? I mean, she's eaten worse. But the vet is always concerned when she does stuff like this. She's so tiny. It's not good for her."

"You should probably call just to make sure."

"I will." Parker pulled out his phone, scooped up Blue, and wandered over into the living room while Chloe poured herself a cup of coffee. He was off his call mere minutes later. "They want to see her right away. They don't want to take a chance." He sighed. "And neither do I."

She couldn't ignore the concern on his face. Normally carefree Parker was worried. "I'm sure she'll be fine. But you're doing the right thing by taking her in."

He sighed. "I was hoping you and I could have a chat this morning."

"About what?"

"A bunch of things."

Chloe wasn't sure what that meant, and with the threat of seeing her mom that morning hanging over head, she wasn't sure she could handle more drama. "Chats can wait. You take Blue in and I'll go have breakfast with my mom. Hopefully we'll both have good things to report when we talk later."

"Okay. Thanks." Parker kissed Chloe's cheek and hustled to his bedroom with Blue in tow.

Chloe took the chance to sweep up the remnants of Blue's Tiffany snack, then headed off to get ready. Parker was putting Blue in a carrier. "Text me when you know something," Chloe said.

"Same to you." He straightened, holding on to Blue, then gave Chloe a peck on the forehead. "Good luck with your mom."

"Thanks. I appreciate it." As soon as the elevator door closed, Chloe grabbed a shower, did her hair and makeup and got dressed. Forty minutes later, she was down in the lobby, where the doorman hailed her a cab. Soon after, she arrived at Muffy's in Tribeca, one of her mom's favorite breakfast spots, even though it was a serious haul from her apartment on the Upper East Side.

Chloe walked inside, immediately spotting her mom at a booth in the back of the restaurant. Her mother always wanted privacy, and Chloe was thankful for that. If she lost her mind over Parker, hopefully no one would overhear. Her mom rose up out of her seat and hugged Chloe when she reached the table.

Chloe couldn't help but notice that her mom didn't look particularly well. "Are you okay?" she took a seat on the bench opposite her mom.

"My stomach is unsettled this morning, but I think I just need something to eat. You know I rarely have pancakes, but I might have to make an exception today. It sounds good to me."

"I'm sorry to hear you aren't feeling well." This did not bode well for what Chloe needed to get off her chest.

The waiter came by to refill her mother's coffee and offer some to Chloe, to which she eagerly agreed. "We'll both have a short stack and fruit," her mom said, taking the liberty of ordering for them both.

"So?" Her mother arched both eyebrows at Chloe once they were alone again. "Are you going to tell me what's going on?"

Chloe took in a deep breath for courage as the waiter brought her coffee. "Yes. I am." She smoothed her napkin across her lap. "I have a boyfriend. It's the guy I spent time with in Miami. I like him a lot. Far more than I ever expected to like any man, quite honestly."

"I sense you're stalling, darling."

She was right, and Chloe knew it was time to face the music. "The only reason I haven't said anything about him to you is because I was protecting you. I figured it wouldn't last and I didn't want you to be hurt by my becoming involved with him."

"Protecting me?"

"Yes. It's Parker Sullivan. He's the man I'm seeing."

"George's son?"

"Yes."

Her mother swallowed hard and her lips formed a hard, thin line. "Parker Sullivan. Is your boyfriend. The son of the man who stomped on my heart is your fling."

Chloe reached across the table for her mother's hand, but her mom pulled away. "That's why I didn't say anything. Believe me, I never planned on this happening. It just did."

"This news is not improving my intestinal distress." Her mom closed her eyes for a moment and pressed her fingertips to the center of her chest, rubbing in little circles. "You realize he's a playboy, just like his father. Goes through women the way some people go through garbage bags."

"That's really not fair. Honestly, I know Parker has that reputation, but he's not really like that. He's incredibly kind and thoughtful. He's heavily involved with the cancer center. He does a ton of volunteer work for them. Real work, not just writing a check." Chloe knew she wasn't making a case for Parker so much as she was making excuses. "And he treats me so well. He gave me this necklace last night."

Her mom looked off into the reaches of the restaurant, then lifted her menu to shield her face. "Are people staring at us?"

"Wait. What?" Chloe turned, and sure enough, several people were staring in their direction, and they all clumsily averted their gaze when Chloe made eye contact. Just then, somewhere from the depths of her bag, her phone beeped with a text. Then another. "Hold on. I need to look at this. It might be

Parker. He had to take his dog to the vet this morning." She rifled through her bag. The phone beeped
again. "She's so adorable. Her name is Blue and she's
the cutest thing."

Finally, she found the damn thing and fumbled
with it just as the waiter delivered their breakfasts.
The first text was from Taylor.

Little Black Book went after you. And your bad boy.
And your mom. And your bad boy's bad dad.

The second was from Alex.

OMG. Are you okay?

The third, from Forrest.

We have a situation. Don't panic. Maybe head
straight to the office after breakfast?

Chloe pulled up the social media app and it was
the first thing in her feed. A photo of her and Parker
at the fundraiser. In the hall. Chloe's breast had a
black bar over it and Parker's hand was between
her legs. She immediately saw there was more than
one image, and her horror grew with each new one.
The second was of her mom and George Sullivan on
their wedding day, kissing. The third was of George
kissing a woman in much the same way Parker had
kissed Chloe in the hall. It was dated, too. The same
day as the wedding. Chloe's head spun. Her stom-

ach lurched. Then she looked at the caption. "Like father, like son. And they apparently have a weakness for mother and daughter. Kinky, Sullivan boys. Real kinky."

"Mom. We have a bit of a problem..." When Chloe looked up, she saw that her mom was staring straight at her phone. And the expression on her face told Chloe all she needed to know. The color in her mom's face turned from rosy pink to pale, and then to a nearly green color.

She looked up from her screen. "The bastard cheated on me on our wedding day? Are you freaking kidding me?"

Before Chloe could even respond, her mom was clutching her chest and slumping down in her seat. Her mother was prone to dramatic exaggeration, but this was something else. Something serious.

"Somebody help me!" Chloe sprang into action, jumping out of her seat and calling 911 at the same time. "Mom. Mom. Are you okay?" She hated the desperation in her voice, but the glazed-over look in her mother's eyes was truly frightening.

The 911 operator answered. "911. What's your emergency?"

The waiter, hostess and a bus boy rushed over. "How can we help?"

Chloe handed the hostess her phone. "It's 911. Tell them everything. My mom is Eliza Burnett. She's fifty-nine. She was complaining of indigestion when I got here." She pushed aside the table and kneeled on the floor next to her mom. "Talk to me."

"Aspirin. In my purse. Doctor told me to take it."

"The ambulance is on their way. Presbyterian Hospital is only a few blocks. They should be here quickly."

Calling for an ambulance in Manhattan was a potential nightmare in the making, so Chloe was thankful for it being a Tuesday morning, after rush hour. She tore open her mom's purse and found the bottle of aspirin and gave it to her, holding her head up so she could take a sip of water to swallow it down. She was conscious, but completely out of it. Chloe took her pulse and it seemed incredibly weak. She closed her eyes and pinched the bridge of her nose for a moment. Between the news of Parker and whatever just happened with Little Black Book, Chloe couldn't help but feel responsible.

Two EMS workers came barreling into the restaurant mere minutes later, asking Chloe to leave her mom's side so they could tend to her. Next came a stretcher and calls into a walkie-talkie, and the growing murmurs of everyone in the restaurant, who were all now standing and staring. Chloe watched in horror, feeling so helpless. She'd never felt so horrible. Or responsible. Or more like a terrible daughter.

"We're taking her in. You can't ride in the ambulance, but you can meet us in the emergency room at Presbyterian."

What a day for Chloe to not have Liam there to drive her. "Okay. Got it. I'll hop in a cab." Chloe grabbed some cash and tossed it on the table as they wheeled her mom out of the restaurant. When Chloe walked out onto the sidewalk to find a cab, she felt so inept. Like she'd been robbed of all ability to do anything. *Keep it together.* She stepped to the curb and thrust her hand in the air. Luckily, a taxi was waiting at the far end of the block, and the driver peeled away and picked her up.

Inside the cab, Chloe realized she still hadn't heard from Parker, so she called him. The explanation of what had happened came out in a blur. A long stream of consciousness that she hoped covered all the bases, including the shock of Little Black Book.

"I'll come and meet you at the hospital. I'm dropping Blue off at home. She's fine."

At least not everything was terrible. "I don't know if that's a great idea, Parker. She had the attack after I told her about us. And after those horrible pictures on the Little Black Book account."

"There's a lot to unpack here, and I do not want you to be alone, Chloe. I'm coming down there right now. I promise to stay out of the line of sight of your mom. Okay?"

The cab was pulling up to the hospital. She was terrified. And she knew that she needed two things very badly—for her mom to be okay, and for Parker to get there as soon as possible.

This was bad. Really, truly awful. That was all Parker could think as he sat in the back of the car on the way to the hospital. Everything had truly fallen apart, and for the guy who liked to say that it didn't bother him when things were messy, everything was eating at Parker like crazy right now. Little Black Book apparently had a vendetta against him, one he'd provoked, which he had no means of fixing other than to shrink into a corner and hope they would decide to go after someone else.

More important than that, he'd hurt Chloe. Only she didn't know it. And he'd possibly played a role in her mom having a heart attack. Things couldn't get much worse.

There was a part of him that had always suspected a disaster would be the final result of his relationship with Chloe. But there was another part of him that had been willing to ignore the chance of that, apparently. He couldn't decide whether it was better to be incredibly self-aware or blissfully ignorant of one's own shortcomings. He'd vacillated between the two for most of his life, recognizing his weaknesses—he didn't believe in love and thus it was best to use this as a guiding principle in all personal matters—and ignoring his shortcomings—not believing in love—made it blissfully simple to avoid ever being hurt by it. It certainly made things simpler. Less complicated. Less messy.

Dammit. He'd been telling Chloe to not get stressed about life being messy. When in reality, it was easy for Parker to adhere to that philosophy. He'd made his own life incredibly uncomplicated by telling himself that personal relationships didn't mean much. Now that he was stuck in a situation where he had to accept a whole lot of blame, his heart was in jeopardy and he knew how wrong he had been. The thought of Chloe hating him forever was unthinkable. It turned any thought of the future into a black cloud.

He knew he had to talk to his dad before he faced either of the Burnett women. They would want an explanation for that photo of his dad—the one where he was kissing a woman who wasn't his wife, on the same day he'd said, "I do."

He dialed his dad's number, but was surprised when his family's longtime housekeeper, JoJo, answered the phone. "Good morning, Parker," she said.

"Good morning. Did I call the home number? I meant to call Dad's cell."

"You must have done it by accident. I'm happy to hear you, though."

Parker would love to have a leisurely conversation, but there was no time for that. "You, too. I'd love to catch up, but I really need to speak to him."

"He's finishing up a workout in the home gym. He should be done soon."

"Oh. Okay."

"Are you alright, Parker?"

"Why do you ask?"

"You sound so sad. I haven't heard that in your voice since your mom left us."

Parker's dad wasn't the only tether to his mother. JoJo had known her, too. "A whole bunch of stuff went off the rails. I'm worried I might lose someone who means a lot to me."

"Is this person sick?"

"No, thank goodness." He did have some things

to be thankful for. His chance with Chloe was still there, even if it felt like it was slipping through his fingers. "And I'm hoping I can keep her. I just have a lot to apologize for."

"Her. That makes me happy. I'd like to see you fall in love, Parker. You've always been so generous of heart. You should share that with someone."

For a moment, Parker was frozen. His brain was going at remarkable speeds, but his body was stuck. Generous of heart? "Almost no one describes me that way. And if they do, I'm giving them money." Although it was true that Chloe had told Parker he was generous when she'd learned of his philanthropic work with the hospital. She'd seen *something* in him. Hopefully she would remember that.

"You've always had a heart of gold. I think it's what made you want to make your dad proud. It's always been your guiding principle."

Everything she'd said churned in Parker's mind. Why hadn't he had a heart-to-heart with JoJo earlier? Like perhaps twenty years ago? "Maybe you're right. And now I need to confront him about something he won't like."

"I'd better batten down the hatches then?"

"Or maybe just stay on the other side of the house for a while. It'll blow over." Parker exhaled. Or it wouldn't blow over. That was his biggest fear.

"Hold on. I think I hear him. Good luck, Parker," she said.

"Bye, JoJo. Thank you."

"Good morning, son," his father said when he picked up the line.

Parker wasn't about to beat around the bush with his dad. "A photo was released today on a social media account called Little Black Book. It's of you, kissing a woman I don't know."

"Why would anyone care about that? I'm single. I can kiss anyone I want."

"It's time-stamped. From the day you married Eliza Burnett."

The other end of the line went quiet. "Oh. I see. Did the woman have dark hair?"

"Does that mean it's true? That you kissed more than one woman on the day you got married?"

"First off, that was technically before Eliza and I got married. It was at the hotel in Vegas. I went down to the casino to get in a few hands of blackjack while Eliza was getting ready and I ran into an old flame."

"Old flame?"

"A cocktail waitress I'd had an on-again, off-again thing with over the years. I told her I was getting married, and she expressed her disappointment that I'd never considered her for commitment."

"So you tried to kiss it away?"

"Not exactly. We went down a hall so we could talk privately and she grabbed me and kissed me. I guess it was just for old times' sake."

"So you weren't having an affair?"

"Whatever you might think of me and my love life, I have never been unfaithful to a woman I was married to. Never."

Parker had never been entirely sure on that point, but he'd worried that the opposite might be true. "Good to know."

"I don't totally understand why you're calling me about this. I don't pay attention to social media, and Eliza and I are divorced now, so that doesn't matter either."

"But Eliza does matter. She matters to her daughter, Chloe, and Chloe is my girlfriend."

His dad snort laughed. "You're kidding."

"It's not a joke. Eliza was already predisposed to hating me, and now it's one hundred times worse. And I really don't want to lose Chloe."

"Do you want me to call Eliza and explain everything? She might hang up on me, but I'll do it if it will help."

Parker wasn't quite sure what to make of the offer, other than he was legitimately shocked. His dad didn't intervene to help others, even when he expected it of them. "On any other day, I would say yes. But unfortunately, Eliza apparently had a heart attack when she saw the photos. I guess it was right after Chloe finally told her that we were involved."

"Oh, no. Is Eliza okay?"

"I don't know exactly. I'm on my way to the hospital right now to be with Chloe."

His father let out a heavy sigh. "It sounds like your life has turned upside down, son. I'm sorry for that. Please send Chloe and Eliza my best. And call me if you need to talk."

It wasn't much consolation, but at least Parker had

a few more answers now. And he took some comfort in knowing that not every conversation with his dad had to be contentious. Hopefully that would continue. "Thanks, Dad. I appreciate that."

Parker hung up the phone and raced out of the car as soon as Benny pulled up to the emergency room entrance. Inside, it was mayhem, but a nurse kindly looked up Eliza's information and directed him to a waiting room on the third floor. One step off the elevator and he saw Chloe. His heart squeezed tight when she looked up and their gazes connected. She ran to him, and he to her. And it felt like the most natural thing in the world.

"What's the latest?" he asked.

"It was definitely a heart attack. They're doing a bunch of tests right now. Best-case scenario, she has an angioplasty and can go home tomorrow if she's stable. Worst case, we're talking a bypass and a major recovery."

"I'm so sorry." Parker pulled her into his embrace as tightly as he could, all while his heart felt as though it weighed hundreds of pounds. He felt so responsible for all of this. "How are you doing?"

"Horrible. It did not go well, even before she had the freaking heart attack. She thinks you're just like your dad, and that's obviously not good."

He thought his heart couldn't feel any heavier, but it was taking on weight like crazy. "I have to tell you something, Chloe. Something that might make you upset."

"What?"

He ran his hand through his hair, peering down into the face that meant so damn much to him. "The photos from Little Black Book. It's all my fault. I'm the reason they posted them. I'm probably the reason they spied on us at all."

"How are you to blame? I don't understand."

"Here. Look at this." He pulled his phone out of his pocket and showed her the text from last night.

All she did was shake her head impossibly slow, but he could feel her anger. It was radiating off her. "You were digging all along, weren't you?"

"Not a lot. Just a little. My investigator, Jessica, is very good and incredibly discreet. And she didn't find out much. I don't even know how they figured it out."

"I can't believe you. Why did you do this when I expressly asked you not to?"

"Okay. Fair enough. I take the blame for it from before Miami. But after that, when they threatened you? Threatened us? I couldn't let that stand."

"Why not? A threat is just a threat. And they didn't post anything the first time."

"Which is exactly why I hoped they would do the same this time. That's why I didn't say anything last night."

"I can't believe you knew this was coming last night and you still didn't tell me. You said all of those sweet things to me and now it's all tainted." She stepped away from him, turned and buried her head in her hands.

He followed, even when he sensed she wanted

nothing to do with him. "I meant those sweet things, Chloe. Every word. I'm not just falling for you, I've fallen. I'm on my knees, begging you to take a breath and remember that we have a good thing. We can get through this."

She turned back, her eyes blazing. "Something always told me you were going to break my heart. And I guess that's where we are, huh? I don't really know what to say to you right now. My mom hates the idea of you. We're all publicly humiliated. My boob is all over the internet."

"With a black bar over it…"

She held up a finger and delivered the sternest look he'd ever seen from her. "Let me finish. And my mom is about to go into surgery or at the very least have a serious procedure, and it was all prompted by your inability to listen to me, coupled with your dad's inability to keep it in his pants."

Parker struggled for words. She wasn't wrong. And he felt so bad. "I never, ever wanted to break your heart. And we have the power to keep it together. The two of us."

Chloe shook her head. "As for now, there is no two of us. There is only me and you, two separate people, who have too many reasons to not be together. We both knew in our heart of hearts that this wasn't going to work. You don't believe in this and neither do I."

"I don't think we're those same people, Chloe. I really don't."

She blew out a breath. "Well, I feel like the same

person. Everything is a mess, and everything I feared might go wrong did."

He reached for her hand, but she pulled it away. "Don't give up on us. I'm begging you."

"Go home, Parker. Go be with Blue and scroll through your phone and find some other woman to occupy your time. I think it's clear that we aren't going to work and I think it's best if we just cut our losses right now."

He shoved his hands into his pockets. "Nope. I'm not going anywhere."

"This is pointless. I'm going to be here all night."

"I don't care. You can't make me leave."

She shook her head. "Staying here won't change a single thing between us, Parker. We won't work. The sooner we both admit it, the less it will hurt."

Twelve

It was a long night. Chloe slept in the chair in her mom's hospital room, but it was horribly uncomfortable. She only tossed and turned, worried about her mother and sick to her stomach over the way things with Parker had fallen apart. Everything ahead of her seemed bleak. Even though her mom had not needed a bypass and the doctors were able to do the less invasive angioplasty, it was a serious situation. Her mom would need her in a way she never had before. The support she'd given in the past had always been about love and romance and relationships. But now they were talking about life and death, and Chloe was facing the reality that her mom wouldn't be around forever. It had shaken her awake to the ways in which she needed to step up.

Parker was another situation entirely. In her heart, she did not want to give up on him. Give up on *them*. But she didn't see her mom getting past this, and this was not the time to push the subject. Her mother needed love and TLC, and a minimum of upset. Bringing up George Sullivan and the way Chloe had fallen for his handsome son was not going to help the situation.

A nurse came in around six a.m. to check her mom's vital signs. She usually slept through these visits, but with the sun peeking between the blinds of her room and the increased commotion in her room, her mom woke up. "Chloe, darling. You stayed all night," she croaked.

"Of course I did." Chloe climbed out of the chair and went to her mother's side. "I couldn't go home and not be here with you." Even though it hadn't been official, home had been with Parker less than twenty-four hours ago. The thought of not returning made her so sad. The idea of not being with him every night made the future seem so dark.

Her mom pointed to the other side of the room, to the ledge that ran under the window. "Who sent flowers?"

"Gavin, actually. I looked up his contact information in your phone and called him. I hope that was okay. He's very worried, but I made sure he knew you were on the mend. I think he's coming to see you this morning during visiting hours."

Her mom sat up in bed. "I'm going to need to put

on some makeup before that can happen. I don't want him to see me looking like this."

"Trust me. You look beautiful. And if he really cares about you, he won't notice at all."

Her mom grimaced in reply and settled back in bed. "If you say so."

"You know, you gave me quite a scare yesterday."

"In my defense, you gave me quite a scare, too."

The nurse was finishing up. "The doctor should be here in the next hour."

"Do you know if she can go home today?"

"It's the doctor's call as to when she'll be discharged. But everything looks good so far this morning. If she's ready, it'll happen all around noon."

"Okay. Thank you," Chloe said, returning her attention to her mom as the nurse left the room. "I'm so sorry about Parker, mom. I should have told you from the beginning." She sighed. "Actually, I suppose it would have been better if I hadn't done it at all."

"You're going to need to start at the beginning. I'm completely in the dark here."

"You mean with Parker."

"Yes. I'd like to know when you became involved with the son of the man who broke my heart, and then broke it all over again yesterday when I saw that horrible photo."

"It all started the day you sent me out to George's house on Long Island to get your things."

"Are you attempting to blame some of this on me?"

"Never. I'm merely pointing out that some things

happen by chance." She pulled her knee up onto the bed so she could face her mom more directly.

"You two started something then?"

"Of course not. In fact, he was kind of a jerk to me. He told me my job was pointless." Funny, but thinking back on that day, despite everything that happened during their first meeting, Chloe could still feel the spark between them. It was so palpable, the electricity filling the air, even when he was cocky and arrogant. He'd taken her by complete surprise that day. And every day since. "Then he got to eat his words a few days later when his client ended up being the target of Little Black Book and he found that he actually needed my help."

"These Little Black Book people sound absolutely horrid. Ruthless."

"Nobody knows who's behind it. But yes, they do seem to be out for blood."

"Someone needs to stop them. Those photos were quite a shock. Why wouldn't you tell me your fling was with George's son?"

As much as Chloe had feared the question, she still felt flat-footed by it. Fear was the real answer, but it wasn't all about being scared of her mother's disapproval. As she pondered her mom's word choice, she was struck by something. "Are you more mad that I did it or that I didn't tell you about it?"

"That you didn't tell me. You're a grown woman. I'm not about to dictate who you become romantically involved with." She wiped some sleep from her eye. "But it bothers me greatly that you hid it from me. We tell each other everything."

Chloe nodded. "I know. You're absolutely right. And I'm sorry. I didn't tell you because…" She heard her own voice trail off. "Because I didn't think it could ever be more than a fling. I didn't think either of us were capable of more."

Her mom reached for Chloe's hand and patted the back of it. "I think you're lying to yourself."

"What?"

"I think that if you were truly convinced you couldn't do it, you simply wouldn't allow yourself to get in too deep. You've always been very good at compartmentalizing your feelings. Of pushing things aside if you didn't think they were good for you."

Chloe had always thought of herself as being almost too attuned to her emotions. She wasn't very good at hiding them, and she was the one who tended to fall apart when everything went wrong. "Is that really what I do?"

"Yes. I think you're trying to protect yourself from the hurt, which is totally understandable. But if you truly believed you couldn't do it, and believed that to your core, you wouldn't have gotten involved with Parker at all. You knew what was at stake. Not only your heart, but my feelings as well, and something told you that you should take that leap anyway."

This was a line of thinking Chloe had not been prepared for, and quite frankly, it stole her breath away. "You don't think I was being horrendously selfish? Because it really feels that way to me some days."

"Darling. You are not the first woman to fall prey to a handsome man. And there's no use punishing yourself for what you've already done. The question is what do you intend to do about it?"

"I guess I feel like all I can do is say I'm sorry."

"To Parker?"

"No. To you."

Her mom laughed quietly. "I just had a heart attack. Believe me, that put a whole lot in perspective. I don't need an apology. I'm over the hurt. I just don't want you to keep a secret like that from me ever again. That's all I ask."

"I won't hide anything from you. Ever." Chloe had thought she might feel as though a weight had been lifted, but the truth was that every problem she'd built up in her head had only partly been about her mom. Any hesitancy had never been about Parker. It was her own reluctance, a battle to see her own potential to do and have more. She was holding herself back. That responsibility could fall at no one else's feet. That was no way to live her life. And she couldn't do it to herself anymore. "Which is why I have to tell you that I love him. And I want to be with him, even if he might not want to be with me anymore. I'm just going to need you to see him as more than George Sullivan's son. Because he is, Mom. He's so much more."

A spectacular grin spread across her mother's face. "Do you have any idea how long I've waited to hear that you're completely head over heels in love with someone?"

"My whole life?"

"Exactly. And it's been agonizing. I don't care who you fall in love with as long as he's good to you."

"He's the best. The absolute best."

"So tell him that."

If only it was as simple as that. "I told him to go home last night. He probably doesn't want anything to do with me. He gave me this beautiful necklace and said all of these incredibly sweet things and I told him to go away."

"Parker was here? At the hospital?"

"He came as soon as I told him what had happened. He was worried about you. About me."

"Even though he suspected that I didn't want him around my daughter? That says an awful lot about how he feels about you."

"Or felt. I'm worried that might not be the case anymore."

"Chloe, darling. There's only one way to find out. And I don't know why you're waiting."

Okay, then. She was going to do this. She was going to fight for Parker. With everything she had. She stood up and grabbed her bag from the floor. "I guess I'll go straight to his apartment. I'm without a driver right now, but I should be able to grab a cab and it's not that far away. He definitely hasn't left for work yet."

"Will you let me know what happens?"

"Of course. I'll come back and help you get home." Chloe leaned down and kissed her mom's forehead. "I love you, Mom."

"I love you, too. More than anything."

"I'm off." Chloe headed for the door.

"Chloe. Do me a favor before you leave?"

"What's that?"

"Fetch my cosmetic bag from my purse. And open the blinds. I need some natural light."

Parker was awake, but he didn't want to open his eyes. Yesterday had been absolute hell, and he feared whatever today held for him. He could finally see Chloe's point about how much it sucked when everything fell apart. He'd always tried to come off as a guy who could roll with the punches, the person who didn't take everything so damn seriously. And for the most part, he was. But the man who'd made countless arguments that there was always good in every bad situation failed to see the bright side right now. Chloe told him to leave. She said that they wouldn't work. And there was no more crushing thought than that.

He rolled from his side to his back, eyes still shut, more physically uncomfortable than any time he could remember. Losing Chloe wasn't an option for him. It simply wasn't. He simply needed to figure out a way back to her. And it wouldn't be jewelry this time, or a trip on a private plane, or an expensive bottle of wine. This project was going to require lots and lots of brutally honest words. He was going to have to spill the complete contents of his head and his heart to her. He was prepared to make a complete fool of himself if necessary. Whatever it took. As soon as he could summon the strength.

From somewhere nearby, Parker swore he heard his name, in a whisper. It was so quiet that it was barely perceptible. And if his brain wasn't operating on essentially zero sleep, he would have said that it was Chloe's voice. That was how far gone he was—he was hallucinating.

But then he heard it again.

"Parker?"

The voice was so quiet. So faint. His mind playing tricks on him. It definitely sounded like Chloe, only he was too afraid to open his eyes and discover that she was nothing more than a figment of his hopeful imagination.

"Parker. I can see your face twitching. Either you're in a deep sleep or you're awake."

His eyes popped open, and there hovering above him was what he'd most hoped for. *Chloe*. His heart broke into a sprint. "Hey. Good morning." He bolted upright. But he'd been lying on a bench in the hospital waiting room, and his back sought its revenge for the agony it had endured all night by spasming. "Uggggggghhhhh!" The next thing he knew he was on the floor on his knees.

"Oh, my God. Are you okay?" Chloe asked, reaching for him.

Several nurses rushed over. "Sir? Are you okay?"

"I'm fine. I'm fine. I just need a minute." His ego was bruised more than anything as he kneeled before these three women, one of whom would determine the fate of his heart. He clutched his flank with one hand and stretched from side to side until the muscles released. He reached for Chloe with his arm. "Can you help me up?"

"Yes. Of course," she said.

Slowly he lifted himself to his feet and straightened, pressing both hands to his back and arching so everything could go back into place. "Thanks, ladies," he said to the nurses. "I think I'm okay." They wandered back to their station, leaving him alone with Chloe. "How's your mom doing?"

"Pretty well. They didn't have to do the bypass. Just the angioplasty. If everything goes well, she can go home later today."

"That's good news. I'm really glad to hear that." It killed him to stand next to her and feel as though he couldn't take her in his arms. He hated feeling so unsure of himself, and like he didn't know where he stood. "I doubt your mom wants to hear this, but my dad does send his best. He was concerned when he heard what happened."

"Thank you. I'll let her know." She sighed and it felt as though his heart was breaking a little more with every passing second. He couldn't endure this much longer. "I need to tell you something, Parker. Something important."

"Yes. Please." Whatever it was, he didn't think things could get much worse between them. Or more strained. Still, the waiting made his chest squeeze tight. It made his throat dry and his hands clammy. He felt a bit like he was waiting to hear his fate, and in many ways, that was exactly the situation he found himself in.

And then Chloe took a step closer and clasped his hand. And his heart spoke to him. *Hold on, buddy. There might be a chance.*

"Parker, this is going to sound completely nuts, but I love you. And I have acted like a complete idiot through most of our short relationship, so if you feel like there is any chance that we can work this out, I want to. Because I think about tomorrow and the next day and the day after that and I don't want to be anywhere but with you. It's the only thing that makes sense to me."

He knew she was talking, but he honestly hadn't heard most of it. He was so happy and relieved that his brain was no longer translating language and was instead thinking about things like sleeping in a real bed with Chloe and sharing meals and maybe going on a vacation and definitely introducing her to his dad. "Hold on a second. Can you go back to the part about how you love me?"

She grinned and tugged hard on his hand. "Hey. Cut it out. I'm trying to spill my guts right now. I'm trying to tell you that I messed up and I hope you'll forgive me. I want to be with you, Parker. For real."

He smiled and pulled her into his arms. "There's nothing to forgive, Chloe. We both made mistakes. Do you honestly think I would have slept on that bench all night if I didn't love you, too?"

She glanced over at the horrible spot where he'd spent his night worried that Chloe would never speak to him again. "It does look pretty miserable."

"You have no idea. My next hospital fundraiser is going to be for better benches in the waiting rooms."

"Don't feel like you have to say I love you just because I did. I didn't say it to put any pressure on you. I want you to take your time. However much time you need."

"Shh," he said. "You're getting way ahead of yourself. The reality is that I've been swallowing back 'I love you' for more than a week. Maybe longer."

"You didn't feel like you could just come out with it?"

"I didn't want to freak you out." It was the truth. "For as much as I was feeling hesitant about us, I knew it was a much bigger deal for you. And I wanted to be respectful of that. But the morning you called and told me about the opportunity for Marcus, that was when I really had to work hard to not say it. I was literally choking on the words."

"So you went to Tiffany."

"Exactly. I had hoped a piece of jewelry could say what I hadn't been able to. And I was relieved you didn't go into a panic that night. Really relieved."

"And then yesterday morning, everything blew up."

"Right. And here we are. Standing in a hospital waiting room. And neither of us have had enough sleep and I know that I smell like I really need a shower."

Chloe laughed. "You can go back to your apartment and get cleaned up if you want to." She turned back to glance at her mom's room. "I need to stay until we at least get a word on when she's going to be discharged."

"I don't want to leave you, Chloe. I'd feel a lot better about things if we could walk out of here together."

"Really?"

"Really." He cleared his throat. "I have one request, though."

"What's that?"

"I'd like to meet your mom."

Her face lit up. "Yes. Of course. That's probably a good idea. Plus, she's going to want to know that we made up. Lucky for you, she's had enough time to put on her makeup. Her boyfriend is coming to visit soon, but she would've refused to meet you if she didn't have it on, so this works out well."

"Sounds like fate to me."

Chloe smiled from ear to ear. "Let's go with that. Come on."

Holding his hand, she led him out of the waiting area and down to her mom's room. The short trip was a near out-of-body experience for Parker. Surely the lack of sleep was contributing to his delirium, but he also knew that he was simply happier than he'd ever been in his whole life. For a moment, he thought about his mom, and how he wished she'd been able to meet Chloe. That wasn't possible, but he would relish taking her to his father's house out on Long Island, finally introducing her to his dad, and of course JoJo, who would surely be eager to give her stamp of approval.

Chloe knocked at the door, then they stepped inside. Ahead was Eliza Burnett, the spitting image of her daughter. Parker instantly knew that they were going to get along just fine. He loved her daughter. That had to count for a whole lot.

"Why, hello," her mom said, sitting up in bed.

"Mom, I want you to meet Parker," Chloe said as they stepped closer to her mother's bedside. She turned to him and looked up into his eyes before she said what came next. "The man I'm never letting go of again."

Thirteen

"I can't believe your mom invited me to brunch." Parker held the elevator for Chloe as she stepped on board, then followed behind her.

The door silently closed and Chloe entered the security code for her mother's apartment. "She adores men, so I suppose it was inevitable that a guy would get invited at some point."

"Do I look presentable?"

Chloe drifted into him and smoothed her hand over his chest. The French blue fabric of his shirt was cool to the touch, but she never failed to pick up on the warmth that radiated from him. "Good enough to eat."

He smirked, bouncing both eyebrows. "Don't get something started in the elevator, Chloe. I'll make the worst second impression."

She popped up on to her toes and pressed a soft kiss to his lips. "Later, then."

"Deal."

Chloe wasn't worried at all about the way he was going to be received by her mom. After the nightmare of everything that happened with Little Black Book, and Chloe's reconciliation with Parker, she knew that she had one more gap to bridge—the one between Parker and her mother. It turned out that Chloe had been quite wrong about her mother's ability to forgive a man for his transgressions, or at the very least, forgive his son. That first meeting in the hospital had gone remarkably well. Of course, Parker had charmed the hell out of her. That was what he did.

But he also hadn't been shy about bringing up uncomfortable subjects. He apologized for his father's actions. And he said he wished he'd taken some time to get to know her while she was married to his dad. Chloe gleaned some life advice from that as well— she shouldn't have dismissed her mother's marriage to George from the outset. She loved her mom, and that meant that she at least needed to see what all the hubbub was about when she chose to take the plunge with a man she loved. Maybe George and Eliza really had been in love, at least for a little while. And if that was all her mother was able to squeeze out of the relationship, Chloe decided that a bit of temporary happiness was better than none at all.

As for her and Parker, there absolutely was happiness. Once they'd both gotten past the horrible aftermath of the Little Black Book posts, there was nothing but a lovely home life. Home, as in Chloe had moved in to Parker's. It was the only thing that made any sense at all. They didn't like being apart from each other. They meshed too well. Chloe had handed over her place to Taylor for a few weeks, who was renovating her own apartment. She was so bored with her job as an events planner that she'd practically become a part-time interior designer, using herself as a guinea pig. Chloe had suggested that Taylor simply follow her heart rather than trying to merely seek success. She hoped her friend would take her advice.

Chloe's mom pulled out all the stops for Parker's first brunch—eggs Benedict, fresh-baked croissants, a simple green salad with champagne vinaigrette, a fresh fruit tart and, of course, mimosas. It would have been enough food for Taylor and Alexandra, too, but they were both busy and had been unable to come. Chloe adored her friends, but she was happy for this time where Parker and her mom could really get to know each other a little more while they enjoyed the fabulous meal.

"Parker, tell me about your little dog. Chloe says she's adorable."

Parker wiped his mouth with the napkin and put his arm around Chloe. "She's the cutest. Her name is Blue. She's a little troublemaker, too. But I love her."

"We're actually thinking about getting another dog. Just so Blue doesn't have to be by herself."

Her mom slanted her head to one side and jutted out her lower lip. "I love hearing you two make plans. It makes me incredibly happy."

Parker leaned over and kissed Chloe's temple. "I couldn't agree more."

Chloe felt the heat rise in her cheeks, but this was Parker's effect on her. He made her feel alive. "We're just looking ahead. No sense in looking back."

"That's right," Parker said.

"That's a wonderful attitude. But I do think we should talk about one thing from the past," her mom said.

Chloe braced herself for something bad. Hopefully it wouldn't be anything to do with Parker's dad. "What, exactly?"

"Little Black Book. I'm sorry, but someone needs to stop them. They're a menace," her mom said.

"Yes!" Parker agreed. "I'm with you one hundred percent, Ms. Burnett."

"They nearly destroyed your relationship. That alone should make you want to get back at them."

"Someone has to rip off the mask and show them for who they are," Parker said.

Chloe was frustrated that Parker wasn't willing to simply let this go. It was like he was obsessed. Her mom wasn't any better. "There's some evidence that it's linked to Simone Astley. That her diary is the original source material. But I don't really know what the connection is between her and the people who are being targeted. And I don't know who would want to air all of the secrets she uncovered over the years. She never had kids. Her entire family is gone."

Her mom took a sip of coffee and looked off into space. "There's one connection to you and I that I can think of."

"Really? What?" Chloe was shocked to say the least.

"Yes. Tell us," Parker said, putting down his fork and leaning forward.

"She attended The Baldwell School for Girls. The same prep school Chloe attended. And Taylor and Alexandra for that matter."

This was news to Chloe. It also made zero sense. "Mom. I was on the board of the Baldwell alumni association. I don't ever remember seeing her name on the list of former students."

"That's because she never graduated. She left school early. I think it was the middle of her junior year. Her parents pulled her out and no one knows exactly why."

"How do you know this?"

"I remember my mother talking about it. They knew each other, and it was the subject of a lot of gossip at the time because she wasn't sent to another school. She was kept at the Astley estate, but it was very rare that anyone ever saw her."

This was getting to be a little creepy, and entirely too close to home. Still, Chloe didn't really buy that there was that much of a connection. "It's probably nothing."

"It's at least worth looking into," Parker said, returning to his eggs. "I have a great investigator. I can have her look into it some more."

Chloe turned to Parker. "No. Absolutely not. I don't know what else Little Black Book has, but if it has anything to do with anyone at this table, I want it to stay under lock and key. No good comes from poking this particular bear."

"Maybe you're right," Parker said.

"I'm right. I'm absolutely certain about this."

"Well, someone should stop them." Her mother poured herself another cup of coffee.

"Someone who isn't us," Chloe countered.

Luckily, the conversation steered away from Little Black Book after that. Parker and her mom had taken the hint—they needed to be thankful that the anonymous social media account no longer seemed to have them in their crosshairs. They could let someone else worry about it. They'd all had plenty of upheaval as a result of having their secrets aired for all to see.

So instead, they chatted about life—her mom's optimistic prognosis on the health front, a few trips she had planned with Gavin, Parker's hopes to sign a few big college basketball stars who were headed to the pros, and Chloe's job trying yet again to get Dakota Ladd to walk the straight and narrow path of not being a kleptomaniac. Chloe marveled at how well Parker and her mom got along. She was amazed that things had worked out, especially after the massive amounts of time she'd spent worrying. By the time they were set to leave, Chloe was filled with nothing but the happiest of good thoughts and feelings.

"What do you two have planned for the rest of the

day?" her mom asked as they stood in the foyer to say their goodbyes.

Chloe looked at Parker and shrugged. They hadn't made any plans at all. "It's Sunday. We'll probably go for a run to work off brunch. Relax. Get ready for the work week."

He put his arm around her shoulders. "Actually, we have a little shopping to do."

"We do?" she asked, peering up at him.

"One stop. It won't take too long."

"Where are we going?"

Parker held his finger to his lips. "It's a surprise."

"Sounds like someone has a trick up his sleeve," her mom said with a distinct edge of glee in her voice.

Chloe wasn't sure what Parker was up to, but she figured she'd find out soon enough. "He likes being mysterious sometimes. I'm just along for the ride." She gave her mother a hug. "Bye, Mom. We'll see you soon?"

"Yes. I need to speak to Gavin, but perhaps the four of us can go to dinner. I'd really like that."

"It's a date," Parker said. "Just let us know when and where and we'll be there."

"That's wonderful." Her mom opened her arms wide to get an embrace from Parker. "I like you, Parker Sullivan. I'm glad that you were willing to stick around for my daughter and be there for her. She really needs that."

Parker stood back from the embrace, but lovingly

grasped her mom's elbows and looked right at her. "I can't imagine being anywhere else."

Chloe thought she might swoon, especially when he turned back to her and bounced both eyebrows. He knew he'd done well, and he was ready to take the credit.

The elevator dinged and the door opened. "That's us," Chloe said, giving her mom one more hug before she and Parker boarded. "Do you want to tell me where we're going?" she asked Parker when they began their descent.

"We're going to visit a man named Mr. Russell."

"I have no clue who that is."

"He's a fairly recent acquaintance of mine, but I think you'll like him a lot. He's British. Very distinguished. Has quite a romantic streak."

"Are we going to his house?"

Parker shook his head. "No. We're going to his workplace."

"On a Sunday?"

"Yes. They're open until seven. I checked. And I made sure he'll be there."

Chloe narrowed her sights on Parker's handsome face. "You're being so secretive."

"I want you to be surprised, Chloe. Life is full of surprises, but I like creating them, too."

"You can't give me one hint?"

"Hmm. Let me think." The elevator door opened and they strolled into the lobby, then out onto the street, where Parker's driver, Benny, was waiting for them. "Oh, I know. Whatever we bring home, we need to keep Blue away from the packaging."

Chloe gasped. "Tiffany?"

"Maybe…"

Benny opened the door for Chloe and she climbed into the back seat of the car, followed by Parker.

"I really wish you would tell me what's going on."

He laughed quietly. "I just want to see if anything catches your eye."

"Anything in particular?"

He leaned closer and nuzzled her neck with his heavenly lips, then whispered in her ear. "I'd like to pick out something that says we're going to be to-gether forever."

* * * * *

*Don't miss other exciting romances
by Karen Booth:*

Best Laid Wedding Plans
Blue Collar Billionaire
All He Wants for Christmas
High Society Secrets
Once Forbidden, Twice Tempted

Available from Harlequin Desire!

WE HOPE YOU ENJOYED
THIS BOOK FROM

HARLEQUIN
DESIRE

*Luxury, scandal, desire—welcome to
the lives of the American elite.*

Be transported to the worlds of oil barons, family dynasties,
moguls and celebrities. Get ready for juicy plot twists,
delicious sensuality and intriguing scandal.

6 NEW BOOKS AVAILABLE EVERY MONTH!

#2857 THE REBEL'S RETURN

Texas Cattleman's Club: Fathers and Sons • by Nadine Gonzalez

Eve Martin has one goal—find her nephew's father—and her unlikely ally is hotelier Rafael Wentworth, who's just returned to Texas and the family who abandoned him. Soon she's falling hard for the playboy in spite of their differences...and their secrets.

#2858 SECRETS OF A BAD REPUTATION

Dynasties: DNA Dilemma • by Joss Wood

Musician Griff O'Hare uses his bad-boy persona to keep others at bay. But when he's booked by straitlaced Kinga Ryder-White for her family's gala, he can't ignore their attraction. Yet as they fall for one another, everything around them falls apart...

#2859 HUSBAND IN NAME ONLY

Gambling Men • by Barbara Dunlop

Everyone believes ambitious Adeline Cambridge and rugged Alaskan politician Joe Breckenridge make a good match. So after one unexpected night and a baby on the way, their families push them into marriage. But will the convenient arrangement withstand the sparks and secrets between them?

#2860 EVER AFTER EXES

Titans of Tech • by Susannah Erwin

Dating app creator Will Taylor makes happily-ever-afters but remains a bachelor after his heart was broken by Finley Smythe. Reunited at a remote resort, they strike an uneasy truce after being stranded together. The attraction's still there even as their complicated past threatens everything...

#2861 ONE NIGHT CONSEQUENCE

Clashing Birthrights • by Yvonne Lindsay

As the widow of his best friend, Stevie Nickerson should be off-limits to CEO Fletcher Richmond, but there's a spark neither can ignore. When he learns she's pregnant, he insists on marriage, but Stevie relishes her independence. Can the two make it work?

#2862 THE WEDDING DARE

Destination Wedding • by Katherine Garbera

After learning a life-shattering secret, entrepreneur Logan Bisset finds solace in the arms of his ex, Quinn Murray. Meeting again at a Nantucket wedding, the heat's still there. But he might lose her again if he can't put the past behind him...

HDCNM0122B

SPECIAL EXCERPT FROM

⊕ HARLEQUIN
DESIRE

*Alaskan senator Jessup Outlaw needs an escape...
and he finds just what he needs on his Napa Valley
vacation: actress Paige Novak. What starts as a fling
soon gets serious, but a familiar face from Paige's past
may ruin everything...*

Read on for a sneak peek of
What Happens on Vacation…
by New York Times *bestselling author Brenda Jackson.*

"Hey, aren't you going to join me?" Paige asked, pushing wet hair back from her face and treading water in the center of the pool. "Swimming is on my list of fun things. We might as well kick things off with a bang."

Bang? Why had she said that? Lust immediately took over his senses. Desire beyond madness consumed him. He was determined that by the time they parted ways at the end of the month their sexual needs, wants and desires would be fulfilled and under control.

Quickly removing his shirt, Jess's hands went to his zipper, inched it down and slid the pants, along with his briefs, down his legs. He knew Paige was watching him and he was glad that he was the man she wanted.

"Come here, Paige."

She smiled and shook her head. "If you want me, Jess, you have to come and get me." She then swam to the far end of the pool, away from him.

Oh, so now she wanted to play hard to get? He had no problem going after her. Maybe now was a good time to tell her that not only had he been captain of his dog sled team, but he'd also been captain of his college swim team.

He glided through the water like an Olympic swimmer going after the gold, and it didn't take long to reach her. When she saw him getting close, she laughed and swam to the other side. Without missing a stroke or losing speed, he did a freestyle flip turn and reached out and caught her by the ankles. The capture was swift and the minute he touched her, more desire rammed through him to the point where water couldn't cool him down.

"I got you," he said, pulling her toward him and swimming with her in his arms to the edge of the pool.

When they reached the shallow end, he allowed her to stand, and the minute her feet touched the bottom she circled her arms around his neck. "No, Jess, I got you and I'm ready for you." Then she leaned in and took his mouth.

Don't miss what happens next in...
What Happens on Vacation...
by Brenda Jackson, the next book in her
Westmoreland Legacy: The Outlaws series!

Available March 2022 wherever
Harlequin Desire books and ebooks are sold.

Harlequin.com

IF YOU ENJOYED THIS BOOK
WE THINK YOU WILL ALSO LOVE

HARLEQUIN
ROMANTIC
SUSPENSE

Danger. Passion. Drama.

These heart-racing page-turners will keep you guessing to the very end. Experience the thrill of unexpected plot twists and irresistible chemistry.

4 NEW BOOKS AVAILABLE EVERY MONTH!

SPECIAL EXCERPT FROM

Ⓗ HARLEQUIN
ROMANTIC SUSPENSE

Interim police chief Marcus Price is captivated by newcomer Erin McGarry, who has come to Knoware to help her sick sister. But he has his hands full with a string of robberies and a credible terrorist threat, and he's not confident that Erin didn't bring the danger to the small community or that either one of them will survive it.

Read on for a sneak preview of
Trouble in Blue,
the next thrilling romance in Beverly Long's Heroes of the Pacific Northwest series!

Marcus watched as she got to her feet. He was grateful to see that she was steady.

"Can we have a minute?" Marcus asked Blade.

"Yeah. Hang on to her good arm," his friend replied. Then he walked away, taking Dawson with him.

"What?" she asked, offering him a sweet smile.

"I'm going to find who did this. I promise you. And you're going to be okay. Jamie Weathers is the best emergency physician this side of the Colorado River. Hell, this side of the Missouri River. He'll fix you up. But don't leave the hospital until you hear from me. You understand?"

"I got it," she said. "I'm going to be fine. It's all going to be fine. I barely had twenty bucks in my bag. He didn't even get my phone. I had that in my back pocket. Nor my keys. Those were in my hand. So he basically got nothing except the cash and my driver's license."

Things didn't matter. "You want me to let Brian and Morgan know?"

"Oh, God, no. Please don't do that." She looked panicked. "Morgan can't have stress right now. I'm grateful that her room is on the other side of the building. Otherwise, she could be watching this spectacle."

They would want to know. But it was her decision. And she was in pain. "Okay," he said, giving in easily.

"Thank you," she said.

"Go get fixed up. I'll talk to you soon."

She nodded.

"And, Erin…" he added.

"Yeah."

"I'm really glad that you're okay."

Don't miss
Trouble in Blue *by Beverly Long,*
available March 2022 wherever
Harlequin Romantic Suspense
books and ebooks are sold.

Harlequin.com